Ms. Stepha

"My story is no fairy tale, but
I believe in happy endings!"

Blessings,
Nina
Marie

CONFESSIONS OF A
HOusEwiFE
INSPIRED BY TRUE EVENTS

SECRETS SHE COULD NO LONGER KEEP

TINA MARIE

Book Cover Models:
Mr. & Mrs. Carl P. Pollard
Tales by Tina Marie
love@mztinamarie.com

Book Cover Photo:
Brandi Davis
Ten 100 Media
ten100mediabookings@gmail.com

Book Cover Design:
Sherilyn Michelle Bennett
Camden Lane Creative Agency
sherilynmichelle@gmail.com

ISBN: 978-1-6847-0122-3 (sc)
ISBN: 978-1-6847-0121-6 (e)

Lulu Publishing Services rev. date: 04/23/2019

Acknowledgements

Carl: My loving, kind and supportive husband without your love and support over these 23 years, I would not be the AMAZING wife who calls you "Daddy" (lol). Love you so much and thank you for loving me more!

Rose Marie: My beautiful, humble and strong Mama your love for me, and your belief in me since birth that has kept me striving to make you proud. Thank you for everything you have ever done for me and I love you more than words can ever express!

My Siblings: Quentin, Askia, Amber and Emonty I thank God for each of you and I love y'all and all my nieces and nephews.

My Family & Friends – Please know that each of you are special to me and have helped me on this journey of life in one way or another. Thank you for your love and support over the years.

God bless each of you and remember
#iSLAY(Seriously Love All Y'all)

Rest in Heaven:

Steven G. Smith
Wayne Pollard, Sr.
Ruby L. Cain
Joe K. Cain
Stanley Davis

Contents

Prologue

I have carried pain, anger, shame, guilt, and bitterness so long I became numb and emotionless. For years, I have been my own worst enemy and waged war against myself. Without warning, my daydreams became nightmares, my ambition turned into manipulation, and my thoughts were cold calculated schemes. My years of being a sweet little girl who longed to hear a lullaby from her daddy at bedtime or make castles in the sand with her Mama would never happen. Poverty, racism, incarceration, bullying, drug smuggling, molestation, rape, drug/alcohol abuse, and hustling, tried to define my life as early as age nine.

I was born and raised in a very small city where the entire inner city is a ghetto, oppression is real, poverty state of mind is a way of thinking, and drugs, alcohol, crime and incarceration is everyday life. The majority of the black people in the inner city are hustlers and gangsters with a felony attached to their name. Oh it gets worst…it's a place where incest, molestation, rape and other malicious acts of violence occur on a regular basis, and go unnoticed because parents are either incarcerated, battling drug and alcohol addictions, or they just simply give up hope, so now the streets are raising the young people. Sadly, this generational cycle continues to repeat itself to the point the city feels cursed by a dark cloud lurking about day in and day out.

There is no longer a sense of community and blacks won't support each other because the presence of oppression, black on black crime, and economic decline has created a "crabs in the bucket" mentality, and each one is clawing at the other trying to get ahead, get on top, or get out of the bucket. Segregation still exists and separates the city, all blacks, Hispanics and other ethnicities on the east side, and whites on the west side. Education is undervalued and it seems the only expectation is a high school diploma or at the least a GED. Some people don't expect either because the most respected position is in the streets where hustlers and gangsters are considered a BOSS and everyone looks up to them because truth be told, they are the ones who run the city.

In this city, if you are not street smart, you will never survive. It is a DOG eat DOG city, filled with many depraved souls. Gun gangsters have replaced gangs and it does not matter if we're related or even if we have the same skin tone, if there is a hint of disrespect, or if you have something these gun gangsters want, their guns give them the power to take whatever they want from you, including your life. In our very small and dangerous city, moving in **SILENCE** must become a skill.

Cherry tops and tomatoes heads aka the police are gangsters in blue and they will violate you or kill you for interference with their corruption. Racial profiling is simply defined as; if you are black, you are a criminal. While still in my Mama's womb, my family experienced the wrath of the police when the police in the middle of the night shot up my Granny's house while she and her family were asleep. The shooting was so bad to the point; my Granny had to find another residence immediately following the shooting. In addition, when I was a teenager, the police entered into the home of my Mama's good friend and killed him in cold blood.

Years later, I visited the city for a weekend and, I was pulled over by the police because they allegedly received a call that my friend who was riding with me had a gun.

After pulling me over, the police put my friend in the back of the police car and in the meantime, I was told to step out of my car and to put my hands on top of the car. During this time, a male officer inappropriately searched my entire body, and by the time his search was complete, I felt totally violated.

My mind began to recall so many visions from my past, my stomach was sick, my heart was beating so fast, tears rolled down my face, and I nearly pissed on myself. I was so full of rage by how this dirty, perverted man abused his power at my expense. No ticket, no arrest, no explanation, just free feels all over the pretty black girl in a red cavalier. My name is Miracle Carter and I believe in God, I believe in love and I believe in confessions.

Welcome to Confessions of a **HOusEwife!**

Confession #1:

Penny Candy

One of my favorite pastimes growing up in the hood is sitting on the porch in the summer. I especially enjoyed sitting on my Granny Carter's porch on the hot summer nights when she lived on the corner of Weadock/Lapeer. I would sit on her porch for hours watching the sexy women work that corner. The grownups thought I was too young to understand what kind of work those women were doing, but I started ear hustling at a very young age, so I had an idea of what was going on. I loved looking at the sexy clothes and heels, the hairstyles and wigs fascinated me as well. Every night when the sunset, I knew it was time to snack on my penny candy and watch my own personal fashion show. I am not sure which intrigued me the most, the way the women dressed or the fancy cars that pulled up night after night to pick the women up, either way, I was taking in all into my mental notes.

Most nights usually three or four women worked the corner of Weadock/Lapeer but there was one woman who stood out from the rest. She was so pretty and her skin was perfect caramel, like coffee look once you put cream in it. She was always dressed well and much more sophisticated than the other ladies and you could tell her hair was natural and her body was just like the song Brick House; thirty six, twenty four, thirty six and yes she was a winning hand, so that's the name I gave her...

Brickhouse. I made up in my mind that Brickhouse was the BOSS and the other women must work for her, and that was reason enough for me to meet her. I had so many questions about what I saw happening night after night on the corner of Weadock/Lapeer. I was only six years old about to turn seven at the time so it's safe to say I wasn't looking for a job, I just wanted to know if she was the BOSS and how did she end up working on the corner of Weadock/Lapeer.

It was in the summer of 1974, when I took a quick trip to our neighborhood store; Mr. Wilson's store, which was around the corner from Granny Carter's on Lapeer Street. I needed to restock my penny candy before my corner fashion show started. I walked in the store, and to my surprise there she stood, it was Brickhouse! She was even more beautiful up close and personal. I was so excited and the smile on her face while she made small talk with the store clerk, made me feel like she was nice enough to

3

make small talk with me also. Maybe I would remind her of the young Brickhouse and take her down memory lane with my juvenile chatter. I was staring at her so hard; I did not see the man coming for her, and as I approached Brickhouse, the painfully loud sound of a slap and the instant vision of blood splatter caused me to freeze in my tracks! A very handsome and dark skinned, mean faced man came from out of nowhere yelling, slapping, punching, stomping and beating Brickhouse before my very eyes. He was screaming at her about money. Asking her repeatedly, "Bitch where is my money." Saying things like, "I own you and all these hoes and I want my money bitch or I'm gone beat your ass until I get it. Listen bitch get up, quit crying and let's go get my money!" I was instantly traumatized and stuck to say the least, and I didn't move nor could I speak. All I could do was cry for Brickhouse until the mean man started screaming at me as if I had his money. He didn't care that I was just a six-year-old little girl in the store trying to buy penny candy. He angrily said to me, "Come here little bitch." I could not move, so I did not. He got so mad because I did not come, and screamed, "You think I'm playing with you little bitch, I said come here." I stopped crying, approached the mean man, and he handed me a bloody twenty dollar bill while telling me to buy some paper towels, hydrogen peroxide and aspirin then told me to keep the change. The mean man demanded that I bring the stuff out to his green Cadillac that was parked out front of Mr. Wilson's store. Suddenly I could speak, and I asked him, "Why?" "So you can help me clean this bitch up and she can get back to work and get my money." He replied. Oh, I thought to myself, he thinks I want to know why he need me to buy these items, but I really want to know why he beat Brickhouse so bad that I couldn't recognize her, so I cleared my throat, got more specific and said, "No, I mean why did you beat Brickhouse? I mean the pretty lady, why did you beat the pretty lady?" The mean man just chuckled loudly and replied, "Just get the shit I asked for lil girl and bring it out to my Cadillac." He grabbed Brickhouse by her hair and dragged her out of the store to his Cadillac.

I had to make some quick decisions I thought to myself. Should I help that mean bastard clean up Brickhouse? Should I just leave the bloody twenty-dollar bill with the store clerk and run out the side door of the store? Should I keep the bloody twenty-dollar bill, wash it off, and keep it because I know Brickhouse would want me to have it? Well the way I see it, the mean man owes me for beating up my friend right in my face, so thanks mister, this will buy a whole month of penny candy. Yup, I ran out that side door of Mr. Wilson's store all the way to my Granny Carter's house and sat quietly on the porch eating my penny candy and replaying in my mind what happened to Brickhouse. Maybe I won't watch the corner fashion show tonight since Brickhouse might call in sick.

I was so angry thinking about what that mean man did to Brickhouse, but I couldn't get him out of my head. I remembered how handsome and well dressed he was, and how his suits look like the ones I see on the men at church but much nicer. What stood out the most to me were his hands because they were perfect! His nails were short and filed and they look soft with diamond rings on the fingers of both hands. He was tall and dark with curly hair and perfect white teeth like Billy Dee Williams. Wait a minute Miracle, I thought to myself, why do I care what this man look like after I had just witnessed what seemed like an attempted murder of second most prettiest black lady I'd ever seen! Foxy Roxy is the first! Furthermore, why I'm I thinking about a grown man like this, I'm only six years old! Maybe I should have told someone what happened to Brickhouse but I didn't. I just sat quietly on the porch eating my **"Penny Candy"** and minding my business, because I remember Uncle Julius said that a tattle teller is the same thing as a snitch and that's a no-no in the hood and in the streets! That summer day in 1974 at the young age of six years old, I felt like I had earned my "street credit" by not uttering a word to anyone about what happened to Brickhouse. Far as I was concerned, it was just a normal day at work for a pretty black woman I will never get to know.

Confession #2:

Miracle

By now you've figured out the inner city ghetto is where my story begins. Growing up, I was the oldest of three children and my two brothers and I were born and raised in the inner city ghettos where we attended predominantly black schools. I and my oldest brother have the same mama and daddy, and our younger brother has his own daddy. It was tough enough being the oldest child and even tougher being a girl. Since my daddy wasn't around,

I always wished I had big brothers to protect me from both intentional and random acts of abuse/violence that happens in the hood daily.

As the oldest, it seems I was the scapegoat, and the one who had to look after my little brothers, in every aspect of life. I was very mature for my age so Mama starts letting me babysit my little brothers when I was eight years old for a couple hours at a time, and no matter how many times Mama said, "Don't open the door for NOBODY and don't let any of your friends come over while I'm gone!" I never listened to that part, and I can remember how as a child our curiosity couldn't wait to leap into exploration during those short couple of hours when were left without adult supervision.

As I reflect on Mama's directive, I have to believe Mama didn't want other children around me and my brothers without adult supervision because of negative influences like bad behaviors or dysfunction of how those children were being raised in their home. I have come to realize that some of the learned behaviors we developed during those unsupervised times like drinking alcohol, doing drugs, and sexual exploration had a huge impact on shaping my childhood and adolescent experiences.

In my younger years, I remember being a happy kid who loved to talk, dance, sing, act and perform for any audience. My dream was to be on television as a famous actress. There is not a shy bone in my body. I have always enjoyed being the center of attention, but not in a needy way, more so, in a "look at me, I'm funny and will keep you engaged and entertained" kind of way. A lot of my family members and close family friends always told me how cute I was as a little girl, and I guess it went straight to my head. I think at some point I developed an alter ego in this cute girl everyone saw, because I never viewed myself in that way. Fact is, I always had a free spirit. Whatever beauty was on the outside never fazed me in my younger years. Sometimes I wonder if I entertained everyone at family gatherings with my "over the top" alter ego because I was trying to hide all my pain and secrets or because this was a version of myself that would protect me from unwanted invasion of the REAL Miracle, who was a broken little girl with many insecurities.

When I was a young girl, because of my insecurities, image has always been important to me. I hated the way my Mama would style my hair and how she dressed me, to the point that I would be in tears. I started picking out my own clothes and doing my own hair at the very young age of seven, but of course, I couldn't do anything with my hair until someone else washed and straightened it with that infamous "hot comb" that gave us our "Black Girl Magic." I was born bald, but it didn't last long, because by age five I had a head full of very thick sandy brown hair. I have always hated having thick hair, because it was such a chore to wash and straightened. My Mama couldn't afford the beauty parlor for my hair grooming needs, so my Granny Carter or my Granny Marsha (who was a cosmetologist) would stand in the gap for special occasions and make sure my "Black Girl Magic" was on point.

I didn't realize how dark my skin was until I was a teenager and some of my family members decided it was cool to start calling me "Blackie." I don't remember being the darkest child in the family so why I was targeted for this cruelty is beyond me! It didn't help that my great grandmother was color struck and didn't care for darker skin people. She was one of the first adults to my memory who didn't like me because of my skin color. "Damn, damn, damn (in my Florida Evans voice)!" I use to avoid the sun by hanging out in the shade during the summer months to keep from getting too dark. I was around twelve years old when the first boy ever said to me, "You kind of cute for a dark skin girl." I didn't know if his comment was a compliment or an insult. Either way, he would become my first serious boyfriend who was light bright almost white.

Even though I had snagged one of the cutest boys at Central Junior High School, I was still insecure about my appearance, because I didn't have the designer clothes and my body was less developed than my friends. They had boobs, booty and their menstrual by the time they were twelve, and I was very skinny and flat chest (as the mean kids would say) with no booty at all. I didn't even have my menstrual until I was sixteen, so I thought something was wrong with me. I just figured God gave me brains and personality instead of beauty. I wanted to stand out, I wanted to be the center of attention, and I wanted to be known for someone other than the poor, skinny, flat chest, dark skin girl with no booty, so I became an overachiever in everything that I set out to do. I make friends easily, but for whatever reasons they don't last long.

I once asked my daddy why it's so easy for me to make friends, but hard to keep them, and he very calmly said, "Because you are perfect! You were made in my image from pure love, and folks didn't like me either." then we laugh together at his foolery aka his philosophy. I think that was the last time I heard my daddy laugh, and he has since passed away. My relationship with Daddy growing up was hit or miss and the few times I connected with him in my younger years, he always showed up bearing money or gifts, thus giving me the impression that's what a man is supposed to do for me to be in my presence. I harbored much resentment toward my Daddy for many years because he made selfish and irresponsible choices as a husband to my Mama and ultimately as a Father to his children, but God!

Daddy and I became really close before he died and

God allowed him to give me away at my wedding, and watch me walk across the stage to get my Bachelor's degree. My daddy was one of kind, and much as it hurt me to see him die, I knew that he died so that I could live and leave a legacy that would have made him proud. He loved me so much and he taught me so much about life and about my worth. I miss him every day and he will always be my first love.

My mama and I had always been close in my younger years, but during my teen and adolescent years, I was very angry and bitter at Mama because I felt like she made poor choices, which led to her not protecting me. In my mind and my heart, I blamed her for EVERY bad thing that happened to me growing up. When I was five years old, I was hit by a car and what I remember from that accident was the horror in my Mama's voice and the pain in her eyes as she lifted my tiny body off the street to rush me to the hospital. In that moment I believe the agony

Mama experienced was that of a mother who loved her child, and she could not bear the thought of losing that child, and for many years it seems that love Mama once had for me was lost, but God!

My Mama is my Queen. She is such a strong, loving, sweet and humble woman. Sometimes I wish I were more like her, because she handles stress, pressure and trials so much better than I do. She's a pretty lady and always has been, we're twins in terms of our looks. What I admire most about my Mama is her strength and sacrifice. I will never know the struggles or burdens of being a mother, let alone a single mother. I watched my Mama struggle as a single mother with three children, and I know it wasn't easy raising us on welfare, but she did it. She did everything she could to try and give us a good life as a single mother. She worked, she hustled and she graduated from college. She did not give up and she finally got a good job as a Corrections Officer shortly after I graduated high school.

I'm from a well-known family and we're well known to both the streets and to the police. When my Mama was six months pregnant with me, she experienced police brutality during a raid of my Granny Carter's home while the police was looking for my Uncle Julius. During this raid, the police shot up Granny Carter's home, and told my Mama to go squat in the streets. As Uncle Julius surrendered, he told the police that they would have to kill him before he would see his pregnant sister squat anywhere! This is why naturally Uncle Julius was one of my favorite uncles. My uncle is my hero, and I was his "**Miracle**." He was an educated black civil rights activist who was hated by the police, and that hate put him in prison for twenty-one years to life. He taught me everything I needed to know about boys, defending myself and he always encouraged me to get the highest level of education possible. His prison sentence was such a devastating blow to our family, as he was our patriarch.

My Mama's side of the family is made up of nine girls, four boys, and lots of grandchildren and great grandchildren. My maternal grandmother, Granny Carter was a single mother who raised her children and several grandchildren through unconditional love. Mama's side of the family is a plethora of beauty queens, gangsters, housewives, soldiers, college graduates, entrepreneurs and so much more.

My daddy was incarcerated most of my life, so I would only get to see his side of the family during the holidays like Thanksgiving or Christmas and some time on the weekends when my paternal Granny and my Aunt Gloria (his oldest sister) was expecting my daddy's collect call from prison. Most of my younger years were spent with my Mama's side of the family because my parents divorced when I was about five years old. My parents divorce for me was the beginning of a broken home, shattered dream and many nightmares.

Confession #3:

Street Boy

Nineteen sixty is when that drug known in the streets as "boy" begins to plague the inner city ghetto of our black communities. I know it's naive to think the street drug dealers who pushed this poison had never gotten high on their own supply, but I just don't understand what kind of human being would sell such a dangerous, life threatening and lethal substance to any person, let alone a black person who is a neighbor, friend, family member or CHILD! Could it be these drug dealers saw these sales as a fast and quick way to get out of the ghetto and provide a better life for their families? Did they not realize the American Dream we all aim to reach was built from the blood sweat and tears of our ancestors? Did they not realize they are part of the problem and this is by no means a solution for anyone? I often wondered why my parents divorced when I was so young, if their goal was to build the American Dream. Growing up, Mama would never talk about my daddy in a negative way. She never told me why he left or what happened between them. I just figured he chose the street life over his family. It would be years later when I learned that Slick Rick found new LOVE...in a **"Street Boy"** named Heroin.

Slick Rick aka my daddy, apparently stole my heart at birth, because from the stories I've been told over the years, I was indeed a daddy's girl. Memories of my daddy at such a young age are vague, but over the years once,

I was older, we developed a bond and I immediately understood why he was my first love. Everyone always tell me I look just like my Mama and I agree, but I'm definitely made in my daddy's image. Slick Rick may have been my first love, but Foxy Roxy aka my Mama, was Rick's first love!

Rick and Roxy fell in love at the young age of fourteen when they met at Central Junior High School. I'm sure it was Rick's captivating hazel eyes coupled with his smile, charisma and fast talk that got the best of Roxy. Rick was always a dapper and stylist dresser, so I'm sure his sense of fashion impressed the young fourteen-year-old Roxy as well. Although Rick had a brilliant mind, he was very rebellious during his teenage years, so he used his brain power in the streets rather than in the schoolhouse, and it was the misuse of his intelligence that led Rick to dropping out of high school and into a life of petty crime and ultimately an inmate in federal prison. Rick's family structure and upbringing was very different than Roxy. Rick's stepfather and mother James and Marsha Hopkins provided a middle class lifestyle for Rick who is the middle child, and Rick's three siblings; Clarence, Gina, and Macy. Rick has half brothers and sisters, but since his biological father was not in his life at a young age, Rick didn't get to know them until later in life.

While growing up, Roxy could be described as a sweet, quiet, and humble young girl who loves school, loves her mother and loves her family. Roxy was born with the gift of clairvoyance. Although Roxy is Granny Carter's second oldest daughter, she was the oldest daughter raised in the home with Granny Carter. Roxy's love for her mother and compassion for her younger siblings compelled Roxy to help her mother as much as she could, even if it meant skipping school. During the time Granny Carter worked as a housekeeper for the upper middle class whites, and at the convent with the nuns, Roxy often missed school to help Granny Carter at work. There were days when Granny Carter was too tired for grocery shopping, Roxy would go to the grocery store and push the grocery cart all the way home, which was miles away.

Mama got pregnant with me during her senior year in high school and after she gave birth, she and Rick married. Mama moved out of Granny Carter's house to build a life with Rick and their new baby girl, me Miracle. My daddy worked at General Motors for about a year until he got hurt on the job and injured his back. The doctor's prescription of narcotic pain pills to ease Daddy's back pain would be the start of my Daddy's drug addiction.

It wasn't long before Daddy became addicted to the pain pills, and that addiction led to him experimenting with heroin. Daddy's addiction to heroin and the street life took over and Daddy eventually quit his job at General Motors to pursue life as a hustler and a pimp. Daddy's addiction was the beginning of him going back and forth to jail, so he and my Mama ended up divorced by the time I turned five years old.

Foxy Roxy was now a single mother who had to start working and hustling to provide for us, so I spent a lot of time at Granny Carter's home. During my early childhood, I attended Longstreet Elementary, which was close to Granny Carter's house on Weadock/Lapeer, so I was always at Granny Carter's house after school. Granny Carter worked third shift at General Motors, so she got off work really late, and during the day, ten of her thirteen children, which were, Julius, Poochie, Donald, Simone, Jewel, Eva, Ava, Lily, and Baby still lived at home so it was always something going on. In addition to Granny Carter's ten children, Simone had a little baby boy named Anthony who lived there as well. My Aunt Baby was just that, a baby, so she and Anthony grew up together like brother and sister, and I'm older than Aunt Baby. Granny

Carter has three more children, Lorraine, Camille, and Sam, but they were not raised in Granny Carter's home. Yes, our family is BIG and Granny Carter raised ten of her thirteen children all alone by the grace of God. My aunt and uncles treated me like I was their baby sibling because my Mama still lived at home when I was born. My Mama and Simone were very close, so whenever I stayed over at Granny Carter's, Simone was my primary babysitter, but all of my aunts and uncles took care of me.

Uncle Donald is my Mama's youngest brother and he is straight gangster. I love him though because he is crazy funny and always has been. Well my Mama decided to let him pick me up from school one day. Why? I don't know, but she trusted her brother with my life. I waited at the pickup spot like I did everyday for my Mama, not knowing my Uncle Donald was in charge of pickup. He was thirty minutes late picking me up and I sat outside that school crying my eyes out because I was so scared and alone. When Uncle Donald got there, he was all hype telling me to hurry up because he has some business to take care of on the way home. "What? No! You're supposed to take me straight to Granny Carter's house." I said, but he didn't listen. Next thing I know, we're at some dude house and soon as the dude stepped outside, Uncle Donald beats the dude so bad, and I'm crying and screaming for my Mama. None of my crying or screaming fazed Uncle Donald. As we walked toward Granny Carter's he said, "Listen niece don't ever let no motherfuckin body punk you, and if anybody ever fucks with you in these streets, you come get your Uncle Donald and I'll beat their asses too!" I was too traumatized to say anything. I just kept walking faster and looking back to see if his victim was coming for us with a posse.

I swear it seemed like that walk from Longstreet took a thousand hours. When we finally made it to Granny Carter's, Uncle Julius and his friends Rollo and Jacob were chilling on Granny Carter's porch shooting dice, smoking weed, talking trash and drinking. As I walked up the porch steps, Rollo said, "Girl you look just like your daddy." I rolled my eyes, and said with an attitude, "I look like my Mama," and walked in the house. Everybody was doing something, cleaning, cooking, doing homework, watching TV, or on the phone. I just wanted to sit down and act like Uncle Donald didn't just beat a man to an inch of his life. I really wanted to go to the store and get some junk food, but I didn't want to run into that mean man who beat up Brickhouse, so I just chilled on the porch with my Uncle Julius and his friends until it was time for my corner fashion show.

I sat in the corner and played jacks alone. Watching the young men on the porch made me think of my daddy and I wished he were here to tell me everything was ok. I needed my Daddy to teach me men should not treat women the way Brickhouse was treated by that mean man, and explain to me what I witnessed in the neighborhood store, but the truth is, I didn't know where he was and my memory of him at that age is so vague, I don't remember him from back then.

My thoughts were interrupted by the sight of a green Cadillac, creeping up Weadock Street. It kind of looked like the one that was parked in front of Mr. Wilson's store the other day, but I didn't get a good look at it because I was so traumatized by what happened to Brickhouse and plus I was inside the store, but I think it's that mean man's Cadillac.

A few days had past and maybe that mean man has forgotten all about me, and that bloody twenty dollars, but what if he gets out of the car and come on the porch, I thought to myself. I jumped up and ran into the house before he got too close. I stayed inside by the screen door until I saw his Cadillac ride by, but it never did.

I heard the mean man's voice yell, "Julius mane let me

put a bug in your ear." I saw my Uncle Julius walk down the porch steps out to the mean man's Cadillac. My first thoughts are, what does he want with my uncle? How does he know my uncle? Does he know that's MY uncle? My heart was beating so fast, I thought I was going to join Elizabeth (in my Fred Sanford voice). Then I hear Rollo, say he heard Sweet Willie beat Vanna up really bad a few days ago at Mr. Wilson's store. What? The mean man's name is Sweet Willie and the pretty lady I call Brickhouse government name is Vanna. I kept ear hustling because I need to know if Sweet Willie is looking for a seven-year-old named Miracle.

Jacob started going off about how he can't stand pimps and he don't know why Vanna is still with Sweet Willie after what he did to her daughter and how he's always beating on her. Then Rollo said the unexpected, "Man you know Julius has been letting Vanna hide out in his room the past couple weekends!" Wait! What? Uncle

Julius is messing around with Brickhouse, I mean Vanna. Is that why Sweet Willie wants to talk to Uncle Julius because he found out about him and Vanna, and what did Sweet Willie do to Vanna's daughter? I'm scared! I want my Mama!

I ran into Granny Carter's bedroom to call my Mama. Soon as she answered, I started yelling and crying and told her to come pick me up because I was having a heart attack. I told her it was gangsters, pimps and hoes over Granny Carter's house and that my heart is beating fast and I can't breathe and I'm scared and it's nowhere to sleep and I need to sleep with her because it's a bad man outside and he did something to Brickhouse's daughter. Mama said, "Quit crying your Granny's on the way home from work right now so you can sleep with her, and I will pick you up tomorrow morning." I hung up the phone and headed back to the porch to see what was going on, but the door was closed and locked. I guess Uncle Julius figured my Granny was on the way home, so party over. Dang! I wanted to continue my ear hustling. I heard the TV in the living room, so I went and sat in the living room and watched television with my aunts and waited quietly for my Granny to get home from work. Granny's routine after work was always the same, and she'd take off her work boots, light up her cigarette and open herself a cold can of 7-Up for her sipping delight. I ran into the kitchen, gave her a hug and kiss, and we had our bonding time.

Granny always let me stay up late with her on the weekends I spent the night there. I told Granny that my Mama said I could sleep with her and that she will pick me up in the morning. Granny and I stayed up for about two more hours while I told her all about my day. Like how Uncle Donald picked me up late from school and about the beat down of the boy who lived in the gray house a few blocks down the street. When Granny didn't

I respond, I looked over at Granny she had already dozed off at the kitchen table. I awoke her so that we could go to bed. I was so tired from the events of my day, I just got in the bed under the covers fully dressed to close my eyes, and my Granny politely says, "Baby you can't ever be too tired to say your prayers," and in unison me and my Granny begin to pray, "Now I lay me down to sleep. I pray the Lord my soul to keep. If I should die before I wake, I pray to God my soul to take. If I should live for other days, I pray the Lord to guide my ways. Father, unto thee I pray, thou hast guarded me all-day; safe I am while in thy sight, safely let me sleep tonight. Bless my friends, the whole world bless; help me to learn helpfulness; keep me every in thy sight; So to all I say good night."

Confessions #4:

Tree Jumper

Whenever my Mama didn't have cash to give me for the snacks I wanted from the neighborhood store, she would give me a book of food stamps. "Mama you know I can't take these food stamps in the store, all the kids' gone laugh and tease me," I said. Mama would clap back, "Miracle everybody in these projects is on welfare and you are not the only one who is going into the store with food stamps."

I trusted my Mama with my life and during those years she was my best friend and I did everything in my power to stick by her side, but I didn't trust her knowledge on this because Mama was not hanging out with these bad kids and just because they were also on welfare doesn't mean a thing! They were still going to laugh and tease me if they see me food stamping (lol) and this is why I decided not to ever be seen using food stamps, because that was my Mama's battle not mine.

Fact is, I didn't care if everybody in the projects was on welfare, because in my mind, I was just a visitor out there in the projects. I knew God had a better plan for my life than what the projects was trying to offer, so I prayed and asked God to open doors for my Mama that no man can shut. I really didn't understand what I was requesting from God in that prayer at such a young age. Granny Carter taught me about the power of prayer and she said, "We must always carry our burdens to God," and often when my Granny prayed, she would always ask God to open doors no man can shut, so I just asked God for the same thing.

It was in spring of 1973 when my Mama moved our family into the projects and my Aunt Jewel and her baby girl Calik moved into an apartment a couple doors down from us. We lived close to my new school Potter Elementary and Augie's Food Market, but only for a short time and then Mama moved us around the corner to a bigger apartment so that my Aunt Simone and her youngest boy Rico could move in with us. By this time, I had two little brothers, Alex and Lokey, and yes, all six of us lived together in that apartment for at least two years. My Mama was working and hustling during the day and going to college at night, so my Aunt Simone moved in to help out by taking care of my brothers and I while Mama worked and pursued her education.

I was so happy when Mama let me tag along with her to night classes at St. Joseph College, because my Aunt Simone was so mean and she just plain ole didn't like me. Aunt Simone liked my brothers more than me and I never understood why. She never whooped me, but she was just mean and used to call me mean names. I would throw horrible tantrums when my Mama would leave me home with Aunt Simone. My tears always worked on my Mama, she hadn't realized my acting skills just yet, so she fell for it every time.

The projects was and still is low income housing for the poor and compared to how both of my Granny's were living, we were poor in my opinion. Well actually, the fact that we didn't have a car, or my brothers and I didn't have bikes. Lest not forget we were on welfare, those are all "poor" indicators for me.

There were NO good days for me in the projects! I would experience my first two encounters of trauma there at ages seven and eight. Remember I mentioned that almost every ADULT I'd come in contact with would often refer to me as cute little girl? These were not my thoughts; I just enjoyed having lots of positive energy, being funny, friendly and very curious. Somehow, those characteristics made me "fass" according to the grownup women who I would hear that say whenever I was within earshot. I often wonder if my over friendly "social butterfly" personality is a curse.

My first neighborhood friend in the projects was Sadie. She was a little older than me, and I guess because her family was so involved in church, my Mama felt like it was safe for Sadie to have access to me and for me to hang around her. I believe Mama expected Sadie to watch over me in a big sister kind of way, and so did I, but it didn't take long for Sadie to show me her dark side.

Whenever we were around grownups Sadie acted nice and well behaved, but in real life, she was a bully toward me in private and every time she came around, I was terrified of what she was going to do to me or make me do. Well one very hot summer day, Sadie decided she wanted to take some fresh "doo doo" out of her toilet and rub it on me, and she did. She smeared it on my leg and I just about vomited from the smell and the vision of "dookie" on my body! I was sick and I just wanted to go home and get away from her, but she immediately clean the dookie off me and suggested we go play. Call me a dummy because that is what I must have been when I left with her to roam the projects and play with the other neighborhood kids. Sadie wanted to round up some bodies to play kickball, well at least that's what she told me, because she knew that was my favorite game.

My Mama always told me to follow my first mind (didn't know what that meant until this day). My first mind told me to run out of Sadie's apartment which was right next door to ours and get to safety, after the "dookie" incident but when Sadie suggested we go play kickball, I was all in. Sadie and I were able to round up a crew of other neighborhood kids in no time since we all lived fairly close in proximity.

Sadie told me to go get the ball from inside one of those random isolated utility rooms scattered about the projects. Sadie convinced me that there are balls, jump ropes, hula-hoops, frisbees and other things in those utility rooms for us neighborhood kids to use. No sooner than I opened the door to the utility room, I felt a shove to my back and I quickly fell to the floor and heard the door slam shut.

I was immediately surrounded by complete darkness and a mildew smell. I couldn't see ANYTHING, but I could partially hear Sadie and the other kids laughing and saying mean things on the other side of the door as I pounded on the door and begged to be let out of the room. I didn't know if there was someone or something else in the room with me because it was pitch black. The terror and helplessness I felt is truly indescribable. I just couldn't understand why ME? What did I do to Sadie or these kids to make them want to lock me in this dark room and leave me there for hours! I was so scared...so hurt...so traumatized and I began to cry, scream and continued to pound on the door until I was tired. That room was so dark, hot and quiet. I remember in church, the preacher would always say that God would never leave us or forsake us, and that God is everywhere, and if we need him, all we have to do is call on him. At that moment I knew that God was the only one who could save me from whatever plan or further harm these mean kids had in store for me, so I begin praying, "The Lord is my shepherd; I shall not want. He maketh me to lie down in green pastures: he leadeth me beside the still waters. He restoreth my soul: he leadeth me in the paths of righteousness for his name's sake. Yea, though I walk through the valley of the shadow of death, I will fear no evil: for thou art with me; thy rod and thy staff, they comfort me. Thou preparest a table before me in the presence of mine enemies: thou anointest my head with oil; my cup runneth over. Surely goodness and mercy shall follow me all the days of my life: and I will dwell in the house of the Lord forever." Yes, Psalm 23 is what I called a "prayer" at seven years old.

It worked and one of the other kids who was part of the "let's lock Miracle in the dark room" crew had an older sister who came to my rescue after she learned what happened to me. I was so relieved and I ran all the way home, but my victory was short lived when Sadie found out that I was rescued, she somehow appeared in the back room of our apartment to take me back to the dark room, but I was not going without a fight this time.

As I struggled to get away from Sadie I fell to the floor, begin kicking her to get her off me. Sadie grabbed me by my left leg to pull me out of the back door, but while doing so, my right leg rubbed against a trash bag that had a piece of glass sticking out. The glass cut my leg so fast and so deep, an enormous amount of blood began gushing out and it scared Sadie, so she dropped my ankle and fled.

Needless to say, I ended up in the emergency room and had to get stitches in my leg. This traumatizing experience has left "two" ugly scars...one on my right leg and one on my heart that is finally starting to heal. I wonder why I didn't tell anyone about Sadie and all the horrible things she did, and how awful she treated me. I still wonder if she is the one who set up one of the most terrifying encounters, I'd had in my young seven-year-old life.

I thought for sure that once God brought me out of that dark room, my prayers of being free from trauma were answered until that one day I walked home from school alone. The walk from Potter Elementary to our apartment was a bit far for a seven-year-old little girl to walk home alone, so either my Mama would pick me up, or I'd walk with the other neighborhood kids who lived nearby. Behind the apartment units on our block was a wooded area with a shortcut path that led to our backyards, so we used this shortcut often when walking from one side of the projects to the other.

One summer day after school, I walked home alone. Not sure, why Mama didn't pick me up or why I didn't walk with the other neighborhood kids. Maybe I was impatience, maybe something happened at school, or maybe I was a loner that day. Well this day was no different than any other day except that I was walking alone, so I took the shortcut through the wooded area, because that's the route I knew and it leads me right to our backyard. What happened, as I got closer to the end of the shortcut was very unexpected, when a teenage boy jumped from one of the trees and landed right in my face. Scared nearly to death, I immediately screamed and dropped everything I was holding. I remember him putting his hand over my mouth and I wanted to bite his hand, but it smelled like wet dirt and grass and some other unfamiliar smell I know for sure I didn't want in my mouth. I was so scared and so angry all I could do is started trying to wiggle my way out of his grip. He finally took his hand off my mouth and then he said, "Pull your pants down," and as I started to act like I was going to pull my pants down, I said, "My Uncle Donald Carter is gone kill you if you fuck with me." With fear in his voice, the boy responded, "Oh you're a Carter!" I begin naming every Carter man, woman, boy and girl I could think of, and that boy pulled his pants up and ran out those woods like his life depended on it. I gathered my bearings and all my things that were on the ground and ran all the way home.

Once again, when I got home I didn't say anything to anyone. Why? This was not snitching, this was serious and what if this boy would have hurt me or even killed me. What if he's out there lurking; waiting to hurt some other little girl who doesn't have an Uncle Donald to protect her. What if Mama tells someone and then everybody find out what happened. These are the thoughts that ran through my mind as I sat in my bedroom looking out the window and watching the train go by. I had heard stories about the **"Tree Jumper"** but I thought it was a myth like the boogeyman. I sat my bedroom window so long it began to rain, and all I could do was pray and cry until I fell asleep.

Confession #5:

You Talk Fast

When I woke up from my nap, the image of the tree jumper and what had occurred earlier that day was still on my mind. Somehow, I thought sleep would erase it from my memory. I have to tell my Mama what happened so that she will understand why I hate it in these projects. Nothing but bad things has happened to me since we moved away from Granny Carter's house.

I could smell salmon croquettes, rice and hot water

cornbread as I made my way downstairs, which was the smell that let me know my Mama was home. I found Mama sitting at the dining room table doing her homework before she had to go to class, but I interrupted her to ask if I could go with her to class because I had to tell her something and it was private. Whenever I would talk to my Mama like I was grown, or like she was my bestie, she would give me this confused look like she didn't recognize me, but I never really paid that any attention. Fact is, I was the oldest and I was her only girl at the time, so in my head, that made me the BOSS (lol).

I made a decision to tell my Mama about the boy who jumped out of the tree. Truth is, I didn't want to go to school anymore and I didn't want to hang out with the neighborhood kids anymore. I wanted to go live with my Granny Carter, watch my corner fashion show and hang out with my aunts and uncles. The projects were too dangerous and I have never felt safe since we moved there. These were the thoughts I had as I was preparing my for my private talk with Mama.

On our ride to class, my Mama was jamming to the local radio station, W3 soul, and I was very quiet, but rocking to the music when she asked me what I wanted to talk about. I very politely asked, "Can I talk about it on the way home tonight?" Mama smiled and said, "Yes Love." Love is the nickname my Mama called me from birth until my teenage years.

When me and Mama arrived to the school, Dr. Malone, Mama's professor was there shuffling papers and organizing some things on her desk. I ran in, gave Dr. Malone a hug, and asked if I could erase the board, and of course, she let me. Dr. Malone, liked me so much that on some weekends she would pick me up and let me stay at her house with her daughter Treshina. My most memorable weekend is when I stayed with Treshina and we went to her Dad's house, and to my surprise, Treshina owned a horse. We went horseback riding that weekend and it was the first time I'd seen a horse in real life and also my first time riding a horse, which is the day I fell in love with horses.

Hanging out with Treshina was fun and it was a long way from the projects. I really loved their home and Treshina's room was very pretty. Everything was pink and very fancy. Although I enjoyed spending time with Treshina, I don't think the feeling was mutual. I remember feeling embarrassed sometimes when I didn't know or understand certain things that were common knowledge to the more fortunate. I didn't fit in with Treshina and her friends. As much as I enjoyed the exposure to her lifestyle, I didn't like the feeling of not being worthy or feeling like a misfit. That weekend would be the last time, I'd hang out at Dr. Malone's home.

Before the class started, my Mama always sent me to the vending machine to get her a Coke and a pack of peanuts, and she always put a few of the peanuts inside her Coke. I know weird right. When I asked Mama why she put the peanuts in her Coke she said, "A neighbor of ours started us to doing it and because it didn't taste horrible, I started doing it too." "So kind of like monkey see monkey do," I said. Mama gave me that look I told you about earlier, and I knew that was my cue to stay in a child's place and to go get the peanuts and Coke.

Well, this particular night, my Mama was called upon to teach the class, and since the lesson was structured around writing, my Mama opened her lesson with one of her poems, **"You Talk Fast"** it's my favorite of her many writings. As, I sat in the back of the classroom and watched my Mama teach the class, I was proud and happy to have a Mama who was humble, beautiful and smart, and I couldn't help but wonder how she ended up as a divorced single mother of three children. It was so unfair because in my eyes, my Mama deserved the best this world had to offer.

I was supposed to be working on my homework, but my Mama was so powerful, she had my full attention as she recited her poem. Watching her in this way gave me hope that this school thing was going to get us out of the ghetto. Then I started to daydream how one day my Mama would be teaching a class of her own, and we'd move into a big house like Dr. Malone's and that I would have a pretty room, nice clothes and fancy friends like Treshina.

As Mama's poem came to an end, my thoughts quickly turned to the dreaded talk I need to have with Mama on the way home. Will she believe me? Will she think I made it up so I won't have to walk to school. Does my Mama think I'm fass like the other grown ladies often say? I don't want my Mama to think she's a bad mom or that somehow it's her fault that stupid young boys jump out of trees on innocent little girls. Maybe I can just keep quiet since I scared him off with the threat of my Uncle Donald killing him. Nope, I have to tell my Mama so that she can protect me.

After Mama's class, I was very anxious and ready to tell Mama about the tree jumper, but Mama had to stick around after class to talk with her classmates and Dr. Malone about school stuff. I fell asleep at the desk where I was sitting and by the time we left the school, I was too tired to do anything and all I wanted to do was get home and get in my Mama bed and sleep. Mama kept trying to talk with me on the drive home, asking if I was sleep and reminding me about the private thing that I needed to speak with her about. I didn't want that awful experience with the tree jumper on my mind anymore so I played possum with Mama to avoid that dreadful talk after all. I just wanted it to all go away and I thought to myself, maybe if I just pray and get a good night of rest it will go away.

Once we got home, the gig was up and Mama made me tell her about the "tree jumper!" I told her EVERYTHING! I told her what I said to the boy that jumped out of the tree and I got so excited I cussed as I explained how things went down. I also told Mama how Sadie was a bully toward me and how she would make me fight the other kids for no reason, and how she and the other kids had locked me in that utility room. I told her how much I hated the projects and that I wanted to go live with Granny Carter. Mama was not happy about any of it, especially the fact that I walked home alone, because Mama told me Sadie knows that I was not suppose to walk home alone because of my age. Mama told me everything would be ok, that I wouldn't have to walk home alone anymore and that we would be moving from the projects soon. First thing, I said was thank you

JESUS and Mama followed with an Amen! I headed upstairs to get ready for bed. Even though I had my own bedroom, I loved sleeping with my Mama because it made me feel safe, and after everything I'd been through lately, there was no other place I wanted to be.

As I laid there in Mama's bed, my thoughts were deep and I wondered what my Mama would do with the information, and would things get worse for me because I told her everything. Would the word get out that I'm a snitch? Would Sadie plot to get me back? Would my Uncle Donald find the "tree jumper" and beat him like he beat the boy who lived in the gray house? Will I ever feel safe in these projects again? When exactly are we moving and where? I wanted to share these thoughts with Mama, but by the time she made her way to bed, I was sound asleep.

Confession #6:

Confessions of a HOE

"Get out of my room!" is what I always screamed at my younger brother Alex. He's bad, he plays too much and he's always in my room bothering my things. I wanted a lock on my bedroom door like my Mama room had because I didn't want Alex or anyone else in my room without my permission. As Alex was leaving out of my room, he was giggling and acting very sneaky, but that's just him I thought, so I went in my room closed the door and started getting dressed, so I could pack up a bag and head to my Granny Carter's for the weekend. While in my room getting ready for my weekend, my nostrils became more and more irritated with the strong smell of urine. I began checking my bed and looking around the room and that's when I noticed a puddle coming from my doll collection, which was neatly lined up on the nook near my bedroom window. These dolls were my prized possessions and everyone in the house knew that I loved my dolls, even if I didn't play with them much, they were mine and I was very protective over them as if they were my babies for real. Well, I went to pick up my doll I called Tinkerbell and the smell of urine was so strong I started to gag, so I dropped her quick and the impact of her fall caused her head to disconnect from her body and that's when I saw liquid running from Tinkerbell's little doll body.

After taking a closer look at my doll collection, I

realized that all the dolls were sitting in a big puddle of urine, and without any hesitation I screamed, "Alex you bad bastard, you pissed inside of my dolls! I hate all you motherfuckers!" I didn't waste any time storming of out my room in my t-shirt and panties because I was on the warpath and he was about to get the beat down of his little four year old life.

I can't remember the exact cuss words that were coming from my mouth, but I promise I was speaking in tongues, because I was a professional cusser by age five. When I found him under his bed, I grabbed him by his shirt so hard it ripped while I dragged him back to my room for the beat down. As I was punishing Alex for what he did to my dolls, our younger brother Lokey was standing in the doorway watching and for some reason that made me angrier. I slammed my bedroom door in Lokey's face and to my surprise, he screams out in a loud cry, because his right hand was in the door crack near the hinges and I had closed his entire small hand in the door. At the sound of his scream, I immediately saw part of his tiny finger hanging on for dear life on the inside of my bedroom door.

Suddenly, Mama appeared from out of nowhere screaming at me and asking, "What did you do to my baby?" Before I could respond Mama yelled, "Shut up with your ugly black ass!" I couldn't believe my ears, because my Mama never once talked to me like that, so I immediately shut down. I wanted so bad to cry, but I held back the tears because I knew that Alex was going to pay for it all as soon as I get my hands on him.

Once Mama wrapped Lokey's hand, they headed for the emergency room and meanwhile I just sat on my bed upset thinking about how I didn't get a chance to explain what happened to my dolls and how it wasn't my fault Lokey was careless and how his carelessness interrupted Alex's punishment. I couldn't wait for Mama and Lokey to leave, because Alex is going to wish that he had never touched my dolls.

Alex knew what was coming so he stayed downstairs with Aunt Simone while Mama was gone, and I eventually spent my time alone crying, cleaning up my room, bathing my dolls and hand washing their clothes; all the while, I'm fire mad about everything that has happened knowing none of it was my fault. My emotions were out of control and I just wanted to leave and never come back. This experience would be the first of many that made me the "scapegoat" for every bad thing Alex did and somehow it was always "my" fault!

Turned out Lokey's finger was saved with several stitches and that he would live to see another day, and so would Alex, who stayed out of sight until Mama got home. By the time Mama returned, my bedroom was spotless, my bag was packed and I was ready to go stay the weekend over Granny Carter's house. I couldn't wait to tell my Granny about the projects, the bullying, the tree jumper, what happened to my dolls, Lokey getting stitches...shoot everything that was going on, because I'm sure she didn't know any of it.

Soon as I got to Granny Carter's, I wanted to go back home because it was so boring and everyone was sad. Apparently, my Uncle Julius and his friends were arrested and thrown in jail. I didn't understand what the grownups were talking about when I heard things like, "life sentence," "possibility of parole," "political prisoner," and "black activist." It seems like forever since I last saw Uncle Julius and I needed to talk with him about Brickhouse, I mean "Vanna" and Sweet Willie aka "the mean man," and I also wanted some money for my penny candy run, which I always counted on him giving me every time. Lucky for me, my Aunt Jewel came over Granny Carter's to visit and she took me, Aunt Baby, and my cousin Anthony downtown to get some donuts. Aunt

Jewel was so nice and on our way to the donut shop, she told me that if I do well in school she would take me to see the Jackson 5, who was coming to town during my birthday month. I was so happy, I hugged her waist and told her thank you at least a dozen times and immediately drifted off into my daydreaming state, as I thought about my rich boyfriend Michael Jackson, singing my favorite song "I'll Be There." Hmmmm...I wonder if he's going to bring Ben (the rat), I hope not because I HATE rats! My thoughts were interrupted by the sweet smell of donuts as we entered into Modern Bakery and Aunt Baby and Anthony made a mad dash to the counter for the glazed donuts that all three of us loved.

As we headed back to Granny Carter's house, my curiosity got the best of me, so I asked my Aunt Jewel questions about Uncle Julius and his friends being in jail, but she said, "You're too young to understand." I quickly learned that this was a common response when the adults in our family were keeping something secret from us kids.

By the time we made it to back to Granny Carter's it was a full house, and when we walked into the house there was music playing, the television volume was way too loud and I could smell and hear the sizzling sound of chicken frying in the kitchen. As I made my way back to the kitchen, I could see some women sitting at the kitchen table with my Granny Carter and it look like the women who star in my corner fashion show. As I got closer to the kitchen, I realized I was right, it was a couple of the ladies who worked for Brickhouse on the corner of Weadock/Lapeer, but where was Brickhouse and why were these ladies in my Granny's kitchen, I thought to myself. Granny was laughing and talking with the ladies like she'd known them her whole life and as if they were part of our family. I walked in, spoke to everyone, and immediately attempted to go sit down on my Granny's lap, but Granny told me they were having grown folk's time and for me to go in the living room and watch TV until it was time to eat.

As I started to leave the kitchen, I noticed the ladies who were visiting was drinking beer, which means they were probably tipsy, and that's why Granny didn't want me around, but I needed information. I complained about a tummy ache and my dire need of water, and without waiting for permission, I just went to the sink, grabbed a cup from the drain board, stood on my tiptoes to turn on the water and begin filling my cup. I took my sweet little time getting the water, hoping that Granny and the women would forget all about me and I could get my ear hustle on. Well, my plan worked just as easy as it did when I used this same tactic at home when Mama had company and I wanted to hustle the grownups for money. I heard my Granny say, "Thank you for bringing her here, she'll be safe here for a couple days."

Who is "she," and where is "she," I thought to myself. Could they be talking about Brickhouse? If so, where is she? Is she here? My thoughts got the best of me, so I quickly ran out of the kitchen and headed straight for my Uncle Julius' bedroom because I'm sure "she" is Brickhouse and that's where "she" must be hiding out.

Once I got upstairs, to my surprise, Uncle Julius' bedroom door was locked! Just as I was about to knock on the door, Aunt Lily yells, "Come on Miracle let's go downstairs, it's time to eat." "What about Brickhouse, she might be hungry too." I responded. Aunt Lily gave me a confused look and asked, "Who is Brickhouse?" "Brickhouse is Uncle Julius' girlfriend and the boss of those ladies in the kitchen with Granny," I replied. Aunt Lily said, "Oh." Then we headed downstairs to the kitchen in silence. Her response let me know that she was in the dark about this whole Uncle Julius and Brickhouse situation, which means she has zero information.

When Aunt Lily and I got to the kitchen, we find Granny sitting there at the kitchen table alone smoking a cigarette and crying, so I walk over to my Granny and give her a hug, and she holds me tight and gently says, "Baby stay in school, obey the law, and respect your Mother." I know my Granny was crying because Uncle Julius was in jail, so I just sat quietly while she made our dinner plates and didn't ask any questions because I was sad too. After dinner we all sat in the living room and watched the movie "Claudine" but I noticed during the movie Granny made a couple of trips upstairs. The first trip she had some clothes and the second trip she had a small box and some towels. I looked around the living room and wondered why everyone was acting so normal like they didn't know there was a stranger hiding in Uncle Julius' room. Maybe it's me, I thought to myself, maybe I want it to be true because I heard Rollo say that Uncle Julius had been hiding Brickhouse in his room, and then

I heard Granny tell the ladies, "She will be safe here." One way or another I'm going to find out.

My thoughts were interrupted by Granny's return to the living room. Granny got back just in time to watch her favorite scene from the movie, which was the scene where the oldest son, Charles was being chased by the police, and Charles being chased into Claudine's apartment led to busting Claudine and Rupert's wedding. Charles lil stunt resulted in the entire family being thrown in the police paddy wagon. As I looked around the living room at our family during this scene in the movie, we were all teary eyed, and I believe it's because Charles movie life reminded us of Uncle Julius' real life.

It was late and time for bed. Granny ensured I was bathed, prayed up and was tucked away comfortably in bed by her side. I tried to sleep, but my curiosity would not let me rest, and as soon as I was sure Granny was asleep, I eased out of the bed to finish what I started before dinner and that is to see if I was right about Brickhouse being in Uncle Julius' room. As I headed quietly up the stairs, I could see a light beaming in the hallway and when I reached the top, I saw the light coming through the bathroom door, which was slightly open. The house was so quiet and I didn't want to wake anyone so I went into the bathroom to turn off the light, but when I pushed the bathroom door open, there was lady in the bathtub slumped over with one arm hanging out of the bathtub and it looked like a needle was in her arm.

The sight of this stranger frightened me to the point, I couldn't speak or move, but she wasn't moving either so I didn't know if she was dead or alive. As I was about to turn away and go get my Granny, the lady spoke, "Who's there?" she asked. "It's me Miracle, is your name Brickhouse, I mean Vanna?" I replied. Her voice as so low, I could hardly hear her, when she answered with, "I don't remember." Then I saw the needle fall to the floor, as she was mumbling something, but I couldn't hear her so I walked closer to the bathtub so I could get a better look at her and hear what she was trying to say. I took two steps and she was loud and clear, when she blurted out "HOE" and started laughing while repeatedly saying, "Sweet Willie said my name is HOE!"

Then in a very weak voice, she begins to pray, "Lord I confess...have mercy upon me, O God, according to thy loving-kindness: according unto the multitude of thy tender mercies blot out my transgressions. Wash me thoroughly from mine iniquity, and cleanse me from my sin. For I acknowledge my transgressions: and my sin is ever before me. Against thee, thee only, have I sinned, and done this evil in thy sight: that thou mightest be justified when thou speakest, and be clear when thou judgest. Behold, I was shapen in iniquity; and in sin did my mother conceive me. Behold, thou desirest truth in the inward parts: and in the hidden part thou shalt make me to know wisdom. Purge me with hyssop, and I shall be clean: wash me, and I shall be whiter than snow. Make me to hear joy and gladness; that the bones which thou hast broken may rejoice. Hide thy face from my sins, and blot out all mine iniquities. Create in me a clean heart, O God; and renew a right spirit within me. Cast me not away from thy presence; and take not thy holy spirit from me. Restore unto me the joy of thy salvation; and uphold me with thy free spirit."

By the end of the prayer, she was crying and sobbing, but manage to say clearly, "Miracle that was Psalm 51:1-12, and it's known as the confession prayer. You just heard the **Confessions of a HOE**, now go get your Granny and tell her it's time." I sprinted downstairs to wake up Granny and within minutes, an ambulance had arrived and some white people dressed in white had rescued the lady from the bathtub and carried her out on a stretcher. My heart and mind raced as I clung tight to my Granny's waist, and heard her say with tears rolling down her face, "I love you Vanna Renee."

Confessions #7:

Life Sentence

I knew it! Granny was hiding Brickhouse, I mean Vanna, but why? Well in other news, Tuesday, August 21, 1975 is Uncle Julius' sentencing and it's the day our entire Carter family will dread for many years! While Mama was upstairs getting dressed, Aunt Simone and I sat quietly in the living room watching "As The World Turns", which was one of the many soap operas I was forced to watch, so naturally I was hooked on soaps early in life. I pretended like I didn't know Aunt Simone was crying as I kept my face focused on the television, because we weren't close like me and my other aunts, and I didn't feel like a hug from me would be welcomed, so I just sat there like a good girl and minded my own business.

Mama broke the silence as she entered the living room looking casually beautiful. "Don't cry we're going to be alright because we're a strong family." Mama said as she consoled her sister with a hug. Then Mama gently reached for my hand to help me out of the chair and said, "Come on Love let's go!"

As soon as we got in the car, Mama cranked up the volume on the radio and I immediately started bumping to "Love Train" as the O'Jays number one hit came blaring through the speakers. Whenever Mama didn't want me to hear grown folks talk while riding in the car, she always distracted me with loud music, because she was aware of my ear hustling skills but Mama also knew how much I loved music. Although I could not really hear the conversation happening between Mama and Aunt Simone, I knew it was about Uncle Julius and there was a lot of cussing and racial comments being made.

First stop on the way to the courthouse was Granny Carter's house. Mama had me wait in the car with Aunt Simone while she headed inside the house to escort her mother to the car. Meanwhile, Aunt Simone continued to cry and I partially listened to the radio as I looked out the car window and daydreamed about the Jackson 5 concert, which was happening in less than 60 days! I wondered if my Aunt Jewel will buy me a new outfit for the concert, because the rags I had was not going to get Michael's attention and that is not cool.

As I continued to gazed out of the car window, I was shocked back to reality by the sight of a green Cadillac coming up the street toward our car, and sure enough it was "Sweet Willie," aka "the mean man" (damn, damn,

damn in my Miracle voice). Before I could even begin to panic as the green Cadillac pulled up behind us and stopped, Aunt Simone jumped out of the car in a frantic rage screaming at Sweet Willie, "Motherfucker get your low life, backstabbing, tricking, bitch ass off our mother's property! You know good and damn well today is our brother's court date and you are the last son of a bitch my Mama want to see today!" Then Aunt Simone picked up one of the bricks that lined the driveway and threw it at the green Cadillac, but thank God, she missed.

Just as Granny and Mama were walking out of the house, Sweet Willie burned rubber as he pulled off, and Aunt Simone was chasing after him screaming and crying all at the same time. I cannot believe my eyes or ears, but all the while I am thanking God Sweet Willie still has not found a "Miracle." As Aunt Simone, falls to the ground where she stood crying her eyes out, Mama hurried to get Granny into the car, then goes, and consoles Aunt

Simone while helping her up off the ground and back into the car.

We are finally on our way to the courthouse, and out of respect for Granny my Mama turned the volume down on the radio, and I was all ears on what was about to happen in court but I do not understand any of it. The car is filled with much emotion and grown folk talk, the drive seems to take forever, so of course my thoughts drift back to what just happened in front of my Granny's house between Aunt Simone and the brick, because Sweet Willie did not even make it of out the car. Now I am wondering what is going on between Sweet Willie, Uncle Julius, and Aunt Simone, and also Granny and Brickhouse?

I snapped out of my thoughts when I heard my Granny say, "Take me home Roxy, take me home. I don't want to see my son in shackles!" Without hesitation, we headed back to Granny's house and dropped her off at home. I felt a sudden sadness come over me when I saw tears rolling down my Granny's face as she got out of the car. I wanted to stay with her, but I knew she wanted to be alone with her thoughts and prayers.

We finally make it to the courthouse and I realized I'm the only kid in the place NOT to be, but then again, there's a reason for everything, and I have to believe it was my Uncle Julius' request that I be present at his sentencing since I was his favorite and only niece in his life at the time. As we took our seats, my stomach begin to feel uneasy like a scary feeling and I was very nervous about what was about to happen.

Once court started, there was a lot going on that I didn't understand. After several people stood in that square box, and raised one hand while placing their other on a bible, and swore to tell the truth, the whole truth and nothing but the truth. Those people who were in the square box had to answer a lot of questions. After all questions were answered, the man in the black robe with the wooden hammer in his hand, asked the white people who were sitting to his right, "Has the jury reached a verdict?" One white person from that group of people stood up and said, "Yes your honor, we find Julius King Carter guilty and we sentence him to life with the possibility of parole!" Aunt Simone lost it and had to be removed from the courtroom. Mama was strong but the look in her eyes changed and the unduly harsh sentence her brother received was the beginning of her hatred toward the justice system.

My Mama was hurting so bad but she didn't shed a tear, she just quietly mumbled, "How am I going to tell our mother they gave her son a life sentence." I looked over at Uncle Julius, hoping he would look my way so that I could tell him I love him and that I will miss him and our fun times together, but he didn't budge, and that's when the tears begin to flow down my face. Seeing me cry for my uncle made Mama cry and she hugged me and said, "Don't cry Love, we'll see him soon." Even though court was still in session, Mama and I left immediately after the verdict to look for Aunt Simone so we could head straight to Granny's house and give her the bad news.

On the drive to Granny's house Mama, Aunt Simone and I cried uncontrollably as if someone had died. All I know is that I didn't want to be there when Mama tells Granny what happened in court because I wouldn't be able to handle seeing my Granny broken hearted. When we walked into to Granny's house everyone was sitting around the living room waiting patiently for our arrival with the news, except for Granny, who was in the kitchen sitting at the table reading her bible with tears in her eyes as if she already heard the bad news. Aunt Simone's crying became louder as she walked into the house and between sobs, she managed to utter over and over, "Those dirty honkies gave him a life sentence y'all and he's never going to see the light of day again!" Next thing I heard was my Granny cry out in pain, "God help me Lord, God take care of my baby in that prison Lord, oh God he's a good man Lord, help us God!" Mama and I rushed into the kitchen to help Granny who had collapsed on the kitchen floor clutching her bible as she cried out in agony for her oldest son. It was so sad to see Granny like that, so Mama and I left her there on the floor so she could cry out to God, because we knew there was nothing we could say to heal her pain.

Mama sat down in the living room to update her siblings on what happened in court and the specifics of Uncle Julius' sentence. Of course, everyone was sad and crying because Uncle Julius was the patriarch of the family and his absence would forever change our family's dynamic. Mama was so strong and was able use her amazing strength to comfort the family with her words of assurance that Uncle Julius will be fine and that once he's eligible for visits she will make sure we all support him in every way possible no matter what.

It's been about a week since Uncle Julius went to prison and we're making our first trip to visit him. As we head out for our drive to the prison, Mama told me a close friend of family and her daughter would be joining us on our ride to the prison because they also have a family member who's in the same prison as Uncle Julius. As we bend a couple of corners in our projects complex, Mama also thought I should know this friend and her daughter lived right there in the projects; in fact, not too far from our apartment. Oh no, I thought to myself, I hope her daughter is not one of Sadie's friends who doesn't like me and is part of the bad kids who bullied "Miracle" crew.

Butterflies kick in as me and Mama pull into our soon to be passengers driveway to pick up them up. My first reaction when I saw the lady and her daughter walking toward the car is shock" I was shocked at how "white" they look because for one I didn't know Mama had white friends and for two, white friends with black people hair; or so I thought. Mama told me this lady was a close friend of the family, but I had never seen her at any family gatherings or not even, at our house, so whose family is Mama talking about, I wondered.

The lady approached the car smoking a cigarette while also holding a paper bag wrapped can. Her daughter walked slowly behind her with her head hanging low as if she didn't want to join us on the ride, but as they got closer to the car, I realized her daughter also had a paper bag of something and her head was down because she was searching the contents of the bag she was carrying. I didn't mean to stare at them, but they were both bright-skinned black people, and I had never seen any black people who were light bright almost white, and I had definitely not seen any black people with green eyes. This lady was very pretty. She was tall, thin, and very light skinned with beautiful light green eyes and an Afro. Her daughter was cute, short, chubby and very light skinned like her Mama with big Afro puffs.

After the woman got her daughter settled in the back seat of the car next to me, Mama immediately made an introduction, and says to the woman, "Janice this is my daughter Miracle, and says to me, Miracle that's Janice's daughter Monie." Monie and I looked at each other and exchanged a simultaneous "Hi." I kept staring at Monie and I think it made her feel uncomfortable because she quickly looked away and started searching her bag again. As Mama and Janice got carried away in their own conversation, I struck up small talk with Monie by asking, "Hey what's in your bag?" "Candy, you want some?" Monie replied. That was all Monie said, and she and I spent the first thirty minutes of the prison ride eating candy in silence.

I decided to tell Monie all about how my Aunt Jewel

bought me a ticket to go see the Jackson 5 in concert for my birthday, and how Michael Jackson is going to be my boyfriend. I guess I was rattling on because Monie cut me off by asking, "Are you having a birthday party?" "Girl yes, but only with my family, because I don't have any friends in these projects," I replied. "I'll be your friend if you want me to." Monie said. I was so excited Monie wanted to be my friend; I interrupted Mama and Janice's conversation. "Mama Monie is going to be my friend and she's going to come to my birthday party in October!" I said to Mama "Ok Love," Mama replied and went right back to conversing with Janice. Ironically, "I Want You Back" came on the radio and because Mama knew it was my jam, she cranked up the volume on the radio and for a few miles on the final stretch of our ride to the prison, we all sang along to the Jackson 5 in unison.

We arrived at Jaxson State Penitentiary to visit Uncle Julius', and Mr. George Nelson, who is Janice's husband.

I was ear hustling at some points during our ride to the prison and I heard Janice talking to Mama about her husband George, so I assumed that is who she and Monie are going to visit. Once we were inside the prison lobby, Mama and Janice were busy with the guards that worked behind the counter to get us signed in for our visit, so Monie and I went to the change machine to get quarters for the lockers and the vending machine.

Apparently, one of the prison rules were that before going into the visiting room with the prisoners, all personal items must be locked up, so that meant we could not take anything behind the prison bars, not even our dolls, coloring books, puzzles, etc.

We had to wait in the prison lobby area until the name and number of the prisoner we were visiting was called out by one of the guards behind the counter. There were a lot of other people already sitting in the lobby area waiting to be called. I had never seen white or Mexican kids in real life until my first visit to the prison. The same way I stared at Monie and her Mama when I first saw them, is the way this little white girl in the prison lobby stared at me, Monie, Janice and Mama.

Either the little white girl had never seen black people before, or she was like me and had never seen "white" black people, which is how I would describe Monie and her Mama because of their very light skin. On the other hand, maybe we looked like the black people she'd seen on television, I thought. All I know is that I was staring back at her because she was an odd-looking white girl who didn't look anything like "Shirley Temple." I guess I expected little white girls to look like the dolls I'd seen in the department stores or like Shirley Temple. This little white girl's hair was stringy and looked greasy, and her clothes were wrinkled and dingy, which is nothing like the pretty clothes on the little white girl from the "good ship lollipop!"

Our staring contest was broken when we heard our last names being called, which meant it was time for our visits. I was excited and nervous at the same time. Excited because I really missed my uncle, but nervous because of all the bad things I heard the grownups say about prison. Janice and Monie were called in before us and I watched from afar as my new friend and her Mama waited patiently for the guards to open the prison gate, and no sooner than that gate opened and closed me and Mama were next to go through. Before we could enter the visiting room, our bodies were searched. Then we had to walk through a metal archway type of thing, and finally get an invisible ink mark on our hand that becomes visible once placed under a special light. After that process, we are clear to enter the visiting room and wait for the prisoner to be cleared by a similar process.

"There's my big girl. Come give your Uncle a hug!" said my Uncle Julius, as I leaped into his arms crying. "Don't cry, you know I taught you to be strong and brave." He said. "Yes but I miss you and I miss our talks and walks to the store for my penny candy," I said as I dried my tears. "I know baby" Uncle Julius replied. Uncle Julius greeted my Mama as he hugged her, "Hey sis how was the drive?" "Not bad bro, you look good, they treating you alright?" Mama replied. As we were looking for a place to sit, we searched the visiting room for our friends the Nelsons so we could sit near them and Monie and I could keep each other company while the grown folks talk. I spotted Monie and her Mama while my Mama and Uncle Julius were in their own world talking, laughing and walking at the same time.

This would soon become the routine for our many visits to Jaxson State Penitentiary. Sitting, talking, laughing, and eating snacks from the vending machine for hours at a time, and often taking pictures to capture the memories of our time together. It didn't matter how long the visits were, saying goodbye at the end of every visit was never easy and was never something we could get use to, because there were many times we all cried as we left. At age seven, I had no idea that a "**Life Sentence**" meant exactly that; your whole life would be spent behind prison bars.

Confession #8:

I'll Be There

"You and I must make a pact, we must bring salvation back; where there is love, I'll be there...I'll reach out my hand to you, I'll have faith in all you do; just call my name and I'll be there." These lyrics come blaring through the speakers of my little record player, while I'm brushing my hair and looking in the mirror. Then I began to use the brush as a pretend microphone and I go into full Michael Jackson mode and continue into the second verse. "And oh - I'll be there to comfort you, build my world of dreams around you, I'm so glad that I found you I'll be there with a love that's strong I'll be your strength, I'll keep holding on." Just as I go in for the kill, I didn't see Mama walk into my bedroom, but I heard her singing "Yes I will, yes I will, so I turn in her direction to make eye contact, and we smiled at each other and kept singing until the song started scratching.

"Let me do something with your hair, Aunt Jewel will be here any minute to pick you up," says Mama. As polite as I can, and with my fingers crossed, I responded "Mama I don't want you to do my hair, Aunt Jewel is going to curl it for me because I want to wear my hair down for the concert." "Ok Love it is your special day, so you can wear your hair down, but I'm braiding it for your birthday party," said Mama. I barely respond, "Ok Mama," as I'd already tuned her out, because I was too busy looking at myself in the mirror and admiring my cute outfit: custom made red t-shirt with a black silhouette of little black girl wearing her hair in afro puffs, bell bottom jeans, and red pro-keds. It didn't matter to me that everyone else might also wear Michael Jackson's favorite colors to the concert, because I'm convinced I'll be the only Miracle to stand out in the crowd.

"Happy Birthday to you, happy birthday to you, happy birthday dear Miracle, happy birthday to you!" I heard my Aunt Jewel singing as she makes her way to my bedroom with a bouquet of balloons. "Thank you Aunt Jewel, but my hair needs to be curled, and I want a bang and to wear a headband." I say to my Aunt Jewel as I greet her with a hug around the waist. Aunt Jewel and Mama exchanged pleasantries and the three of us head to the kitchen to make some "Black Girl Magic" happened to my kinky hair. First, I make a stop to the bathroom and grab the hand mirror, so I can watch as my Aunt Jewel style my hair and I can give specific instructions on how my hair must look for Michael Jackson.

By the time Aunt Jewel pressed and curled my hair with a tight bang and added my headband, I had been transformed into a "black" Shirley Temple, but much prettier, if I do say so myself. The excitement of seeing the Jackson 5 (especially Michael) made me forget about all the bad things that had been happening to me, and I was so grateful for my aunt's birthday gifts because it was exactly what I needed at that time. I will never forget Aunt Jewel blessing me for my eighth birthday.

Once we arrived at the concert, I couldn't believe we had front row seats right in the center of the stage. Since this was the first concert, I'd ever attended, I didn't know anything about an opening act and I was getting impatient because I was ready to see Michael so we could dance the night away to all my favorite songs.

It was music to my ears as the lyrics to "I Want You

Back" came blaring through the speaker that was directly in my face:

"When I had you to myself, I didn't want you around; Those pretty faces always make you stand out in a crowd; But someone picked you from the bunch, one glance is all it took; Now it's much too late for me to take a second look Oh baby, give me one more chance to show you that I love you."

I leaped to my feet and started crying, screaming and dancing all in one motion. I looked over at my Aunt Jewel and her smile was so big it made me smile back.

For most of the concert, my Aunt and I sang and danced like it was nobody's business as the Jackson 5 gave the performance of their lives. Then Michael Jackson touched my hand as he reached out into the crowd and touched everybody's hand in the front row; and that's when I had a crying fit because I touched the hand of the most famous little black boy in America! Michael Jackson's hand touching stunt was the concert finale and just like that, he disappeared into darkness, the lights were raised and the concert was over, but I was still crying for my boyfriend to come back.

Apparently, I was daydreaming about all the fun I had at the concert, because I did not hear Mrs. Spine call my name. Mrs. Spine was my third grade teacher at Potter elementary school, and I was undeniably this teacher's pet. I believe my witty personality and people skills is why she always called upon me to help her out once my assignments were complete. "Miracle I need to see you in the hallway please" said Mrs. Spine. I immediately left my desk to go into the hallway and to my surprise, my Mama is in the hallway. Mama was there to pick me up early from school because my Daddy was in town and he tried to come pick me up, but the office staff wouldn't give him any information, so he sent my Mama to pick me up.

I was overcome with so much emotion and the main one being anger because I didn't even remember Slick Rick. Yes, I'd seen pictures of him and heard stories about me being a daddy's girl, but I don't remember his voice, his face or his love. I snapped out of my trans and very boldly said to my Mama "No!" "No what?" Mama asked. "No I'm not leaving school for Slick Rick just because he popped up and wants to see me." I responded. "I'll give you two some privacy," says Mrs. Spine as she makes her way back into the classroom. As soon as Mrs. Spine is out of earshot, Mama starts trying to convince me to leave school and go have a visit with Slick Rick at Granny Marsha's house. "Mama I don't even know him and a real daddy wouldn't be trying to take me out of school. A real daddy would wait until my birthday and make sure I had the best birthday ever since he hasn't been around for any birthdays. I'm a big girl now, I don't need him, and NO I'm not leaving school for a visit with him." I replied to my Mama then I turned and walked back into my classroom. "Miracle I'm sorry and I will tell him you're not ready, I love you." Mama said as I walked away with tears in my eyes.

Yellow crepe paper along with blue and white balloons was the decorations of choice for my BIG eighth birthday party. I was both excited and nervous. I was excited because my family and my new friend Monie was coming over to celebrate with me. I was also nervous because Mama told me after I denied Slick Rick's visit the other day, she told him about my birthday party. Ironically, Mama said Slick Rick's exact words were, **"I'll Be There."** Slick Rick claimed that he'd stick around town long enough to bring me a gift for my eighth birthday. I don't know if he's going to show up or not and if he does, will I still be angry, will I like him, will he like me, will he bring me a gift; these are just a few of the thoughts I pondered at the idea of reuniting with my Daddy Slick Rick.

Turns out, my eighth birthday, party was the best birthday party ever and my family showered me with lots of love, gifts and the best birthday cake ever, and my friend Monie even came. My absolute favorite gift was from my Uncle Julius, it was a personalized brown leather purse with my name inscribed on the front in bright yellow letters, and trimmed with beautiful roses. Mama told me that Uncle Julius had it made by an inmate at the prison who was talented with crafts. I really didn't care who made the purse, just the fact that Uncle Julius remembered my birthday and was able to make it special even from prison meant the world to me. I loved that little brown leather purse!

My birthday party had almost everything a little girl could want except for her Daddy! Slick Rick didn't make it to the party, but I had so much FUN and was surrounded by so much love, I didn't even notice and I also didn't acknowledge his absence and neither did Mama. If I were to be honest, I believe somewhere deep down inside my soul I did want to reunite with my Daddy and that was evident when I cried myself to sleep that night thinking about the fact he missed yet another birthday.

Confession #9

Black Like Me

It's the end of 1975, and the holiday seasons; Thanksgiving and Christmas had come on gone, and both holidays were celebrated to the fullest as usual. Despite our low-income status, Mama always made sure we had great holidays, especially Christmas, and she even made sure we had Christmas lists and Christmas cookies for Santa.

As the Spring of 1976 slowly fades away and Summer seems to peek in, it seems everything in our immediate family is going great! Mama has a steady job, and is getting closer to graduating from Delta College. My brothers and I are doing well in school and we were finally moving out of the projects and into Townhouse Village Apartments, where my brothers and I would attend C.C. Coulter Elementary school together. Mama was so excited about the move because she believed my brothers and I would receive a better education at C.C. Coulter due to the quality of resources provided to suburban area schools. I was excited to get out of the projects and looking forward to making new friends and starting a new life in the suburbs!

Its move in day to our new neighborhood and to our surprise we have "white" neighbors. We barely get settled in and already I get into an altercation with Jessica who is one of the little "white" girls that lived next door to us. Jessica was out in the front yard jumping rope alone, so I approached her to introduce myself and play with her, but she didn't want to play with me, so I retreated to our porch, played with my jacks alone and minded my own business.

Well apparently, my jack playing skills impressed Jessica, so she came over to see what I was doing and asked if she could give "jacks" a try. My first thought was to collect my things and go inside the house because of how Jessica treated me when I tried to play with her jump rope, but instead I thought of what my Granny Carter always says, "Baby be careful how you treat people, because you never know who God will send to help you." I decided to give Jessica a quick tutorial on jacks and let her give it a try, but her coordination skills wouldn't let her be great, so she says, "this is a stupid black game made for stupid black people." Giving Jessica a try at playing jacks fulfilled the teachings of my Granny; slapping Jessica's racist "white" face fulfilled the foundation of my black pride! Jessica's face turned beet red, she begin to cry and then ran into her house.

I noticed that Jessica left her jump rope lying on our porch, so I started jumping rope and chanting, "Five little monkeys, jumping on the bed. One fell off, and bumped his head Mama called the doctor, and the doctor said: "No more monkeys jumping on the bed!"

I finished jumping rope and was about to leave Jessica's jump rope on their porch. A bigger "white" girl, Jessica's older sister Janie comes charging out of their front door and immediately pushes me to the ground and starts kicking me and calling me a "nigger," and in my defense I started kicking back at her and called her a "honky." Mama heard the commotion going on and ran outside to my rescue right at the same time Jessica and Janie's father Mr. Ed Baker came outside to his daughter's rescue. Turns out Mr. Baker is a Pastor, and he immediately apologized to me and Mama for his daughter's behavior and he explained how their family is not racist and how he and his wife have a zero tolerance for racist behavior. He commanded Jessica and Janie to apologize for calling me names, and after both girls apologized to me, I apologized for slapping Jessica and for calling Janie a racist name.

In an effort to bring peace to the situation, Mr. Baker extended an invitation for our family to join their weekly home bible study and to attend his church. I was the only one from our family who accepted the home bible study invite to the Bakers' home, but I encountered a bad experience with their pet cat Daisy who jumped on my head and clawed my braided hair bun, which left me traumatized and terribly afraid of cats, so I never visited the Baker's home again.

My brothers and I accepted Mr. Baker's church invitation, and were able to attend his church because the church provided a bus service that picked up all the neighborhood kids on Sunday to attend both Sunday

School and Morning Worship services. Jessica Baker would become my first "white" friend, and my first experience in developing social skills. Unfortunately our friendship was short lived, because it seems that soon after we (black people) moved into the neighborhood, most of the "whites" moved out of the neighborhood, and Townhouse Village Apartment would soon replicate the projects.

It's my first day at C.C. Coulter Elementary school and because I want to make a good impression, Mama let me wear my new light blue Sunday spring jacket. I was only supposed to wear my good spring jacket on Sundays, but I pleaded with Mama, and she said, "You can wear it, but don't get it dirty." I wanted to show up at my new school wearing one of my favorite outfits which was a yellow shirt with a tan colored lion on the front, and my light blue bell bottom jeans, navy pro-ked shoes and my new light blue spring jacket. When I arrived to my classroom and find that my third grade teacher is a black woman, I knew that Mama was right. C.C. Coulter elementary indeed had the resources needed for a smarty-pants like me.

My third grade and first black teacher's name is Mrs. Falone and has since this day also been referred to as my favorite teacher. Our classroom seating was alphabetically organized and I sat next to Dena Donald who would become my first friend at C.C. Coulter. Our assignment on this day was to write a poem, and since it took a minute for my brainpower to kick in, I leaned over to look at Dena's paper, because she wasn't haven't any trouble getting started. "Let me see what you're writing about," I said to Dena. "Do your own work and write your own poem," Dena snapped back. Dena's comment actually inspired me and it hit me, **"Black Like Me"** would be the perfect name for my poem. Turns out, Mrs. Falone was so impressed with my poem, she had me stand and read it to our third grade class, and she even submitted it to the local newspaper for a writing contest the newspaper was doing, and my poem won first place in the poetry category.

I was so excited about lunch time and going outside to the playground because C.C. Coulter had what I called a "curly slide" and I had never seen anything like it, so I was ready to experience its twists and turns. First thing I did was run to the slide and get in line for my turn to go down the slide. To my surprise there was this short, loud and bossy little black girl regulating the line, and telling people who could go first and who had to wait. When it was my turn to go down the slide, the bossy little black girl asked me, "Are you new here?" "Yeah, who are you?" I replied, "My name is Skyy Jaxson and you can go down the slide now." Skyy replied. "Ok, but I need you to hold my jacket because my Mama told me not to get it dirty." I replied. "Girl it's just one slide, you ain't going to get it dirty, I slide down all the time and I don't get dirty!" Skyy said. Mama always told me to follow my "first mind" and from this day on, I should have listened to my Mama but I didn't.

I went down that slide in my beautiful new light blue spring jacket and when I got to the bottom of the slide, the entire backside of my jacket was BLACK and I was furious because I knew Mama was going to be pissed! I was so disappointed about my jacket, and I felt like Skyy knew all along that the slide was going to ruin my jacket. There was familiar behavior about Skyy, but I couldn't put my finger on it. Nevertheless, this slide encounter would be the beginning of me and Skyy Jaxson having a very complicated friendship.

Confession #10

Big Girls Don't Cry

It's the summer of 1965 and school is out! Our family so far has enjoyed living in Townhouse Village, especially since my Aunt Jewel and her baby girl Calik, has moved into an apartment a few doors down from us. Mama, I and my little brothers have all made friends with people in the neighborhood, and I am officially a Brownie with the Girl Scouts of America. It seems like things are looking up for us and Mama is getting closer to accomplishing her goals of becoming a college graduate and well on her way to providing our family with a better lifestyle, or so I thought. Granny Carter once told me, "Expect the worst, but pray for the best," and it would be a matter of time before I understood those words.

Soon as I thought everything was getting better for us, Mama's nightlife had changed and she was going out partying more, she had all kind of new friends hanging around and she was smoking them funny cigarettes, which I later learned was weed. Mama's new nightlife is why my brothers and I got a new babysitter named Percy, who is Mama's uncle stepson, which made him our "big" cousin. Well, neither I nor my brothers had met this cousin, until the first day he babysit us. He seemed nice and kid friendly, but there was something about his eyes that were creepy.

The night he babysit, he popped us some Jiffy Pop popcorn and we all watched TV together, but then he made my brothers go to bed early, and let me stay up late. I was alright with staying up late because I liked watching The Tonight Show. Once Percy and I were alone, he became really playful and tickled me, but then he put me on his lap and told me to watch the TV. While I was watching the TV Percy was moving me back and forth on his lap and I could feel his private part as he reached his hand under my nightgown and started rubbing on my private part. I jumped off his lap and told him I wanted to go to bed. Percy said, "Miracle this is our secret and if you tell your Mama what happened, I will tell her you're a liar and she won't believe you, because you know everybody thinks you're fass anyway."

I stormed upstairs to my Mama's bedroom and started crying because I was scared and alone and I just wanted my Mama. I was too scared to go to sleep, so I just laid in my Mama's bed and cried and prayed that my Mama would hurry home so I can tell her what Percy did to me, and ask her if she thinks I'm fass like Percy said. My Mama told me if anyone ever touches my private part let her know, so why wouldn't she believe me I thought to myself.

I woke up the next morning in my own bed so I must have cried myself to sleep waiting on my Mama to get home. My first thought is, how do I tell Mama about Percy. The more I think about what led to his behavior, I wonder if it's my fault because I wanted to stay up late and watch the Tonight Show, and why did I let Percy put me on his lap in the first place when I knew it was wrong. If I don't tell Mama, she will probably have Percy babysit us again, and he might do something worse than he did last night, or do something to my brothers.

My thoughts got the best of me, so I went to knock on Mama's bedroom door. I needed to tell her everything that happened last night, but instead of inviting me into her bedroom, Mama yelled, "Miracle get you and your brothers ready for camp and you can fix y'all some cereal for breakfast; and don't forget to lock the door and your way out for camp." I did what I was told, got dressed and got my brothers dressed, fed the two of them cereal because I didn't want anything to eat, and then the three of us headed out for day camp.

As I walked with my brothers to camp, many thoughts went through my mind about the incident with Percy and thinking about it made me feel funny inside, like a bad person with a horrible secret and all I wanted to do is forget about it and pray that I never think about it again. I remember Granny Carter told me if you tell anyone something private it's no longer a secret, but if you confess it to God He will forgive you. So that's it I thought, I'll asked God to forgive me for sitting on Percy's lap and for not telling my Mama about this horrible thing and it will all go away.

Day camp let out early so my brothers and I headed

straight home to get ready for the weekend. When we arrived home and walked into the living room, there's a strange yet familiar looking man sitting on our couch, and before anyone could speak, the stranger leaps to his feet while looking at me and says, "Tinki you remember me?" "Rick she doesn't remember that nickname." Mama said to the man, however, he pays Mama no attention and he picks up me, swings me around and said, "Look at Daddy's big girl, where did my little Tinki go!" The cat was out the bag...the stranger is my Daddy! I show no emotion when I say firmly, "Put me down!" The minute my feet touched the floor I ran upstairs to my bedroom with tears in my eyes, anger in my heart, and outrage in my soul. My emotions were out of control and I wasn't strong enough to stay and ask Rick to his face these questions."Where were you when that mean man disrespected me in the corner store?" "Where were you when Sadie and those other kids bullied me in the projects?" "Where were you when that boy jumped out the tree to rape me?" "Where were you when Percy put me on his lap and was touching on my private area?" "Hell, where have you been these past eight years of my life?" None of these thoughts or emotions made me feel like a Daddy's girl, and far as I was concerned there was no love lost between me and Slick Rick aka my Daddy!

Alone in my bedroom, as I dried my tears, and looked at my reflection in the mirror, I began reciting the first few lines of my winning poem "Black Like Me" and it goes:

"Black like me, black like me

Oh my what it means to be black like me;

Black is my race and black is my skin

Black is the world that I live in."

Black is beautiful and many shades are we;

Black is who I am, strong and smart is who I be."

As I continued to stare at my reflection in the mirror, I instinctively snapped into survival mode and prepared myself to go back downstairs and formally introduce myself to the stranger in our living room wearing the fancy clothes and fancy jewelry.

As I made my way into the living room, I see that Rick had already begin bonding with Alex, and to break the awkwardness I said, "He looks just like you, and I look just like my Mama." "Miracle you are a beautiful little girl, come give your Daddy a hug." said Rick. As I approach Rick, of course I'm checking him out from head to toe, and from head to toe he's casket sharp, and has the prettiest brown eyes I've ever seen on a black man, which makes him very attractive. I can't help but stare at Rick searching for a piece of me in him, something to make a connection and remind me of the love we once shared, but there's nothing. "Hey let me take you and your brother for ice cream." Said Rick. "Ok, I love ice cream." I replied as I accepted Rick's invitation. Rick's car is as fancy as his clothes and jewelry, and I'm excited to see the inside of it, so I can crank the radio volume and ride in style.

As we drove toward the entrance of Townhouse Village, Rick pulls over to the side of the road and said, "Come here Miracle and sit on Daddy's lap!" My entire body begins to tremble and tears flowed uncontrollably down my face as I looked around searching for help, and Rick yells, "Stop all that damn crying, big girls don't cry, now come over here and sit on my lap so I can teach you how to drive!" "I'm only eight years old I don't want to drive and I don't want to sit on your lap!" I cried out. I was crying so hard for my Mama because I was terrified of Rick's intentions. Rick didn't care about my tears, he grabbed me and sat me on his lap. Within in minutes, of sitting on Rick's lap, his gentle approach in helping me place my hands on the steering wheel, and showing me how to shift the car into gear, calmed me down because I realized he was really teaching me how to drive at eight-years old.

I listened attentively to my Daddy's voice as he instructed me on how to drive his car through Bloomfield's neighborhood until I crashed into a mailbox. In that moment me, Rick and Alex broke our silence with laughter at the exact same time and the exact same laugh, and that's when I found a piece of me in Rick, who was no longer known to me as the stranger in fancy clothes and fancy jewelry he was indeed my Daddy!

I guess me running into that mailbox made Daddy nervous, so he immediately took over the drive to rush me and Alex back home. I thought he'd forgotten all about the our ice cream date until he pulled into our parking space and parked long enough to pull out the biggest wad of money I'd ever seen, and gave me and Alex two hundred dollars each. I was so happy and excited that before I realized it, I hugged my Daddy, told him I loved him and asked him when will we see him again. "I love you to Miracle, take care of your brother and I'll see y'all again soon." Daddy said as he pulled off in his fancy car. My spirit told me it would be a very long time before I see my Daddy again, but I didn't cry as he drove away because Daddy said, **"Big Girls Don't Cry!"**

Confession #11

The Picture Man

Its fall of 1976 and the good news is Granny Carter purchased her first home in "The Woods" on Collingwood to be exact, which was not too far from the fairground. Going to the county fair was a family tradition that I looked forward to every year just before school started. I was so happy and proud of my Granny Carter for buying a new home and upgrading to a new neighborhood for her and the family. My memories will always hold my fun times on Weadock/Lapeer and my summer nights sitting on the porch snacking on my penny candy while watching my corner fashion show, and hanging out with Uncle Julius.

Just thinking about Weadock/Lapeer, I'm reminded of Brickhouse and what happened the last time I saw her at the old house. I can't help but wonder if she survived her attempted overdose and if she still works on the corner of Weadock/Lapeer and if she's still with that mean man Sweet Willie. I guess I will never get to know my friend who called herself a **"HOE"** that I now know as Vanna Renee aka Brickhouse.

It's my first weekend sleepover at Granny Carter's new house and I was so excited about going to the county fair, because it was the first time I'd be hanging out with my aunts Ava and Eva, and with the fairground being so close we all decided to walk to the fair. As me, Ava, Eva, Lily, and Baby walked into the county fair together some random girl rolled her eyes at us and said, "Them Carters," but before she could finish what she was saying, Ava and Eva cut her off and said in unison, "Them Carters what trick...don't start none won't be none!" Then right before my eyes about three other girls appeared, who were apparently friends of Ava and Eva and they all started walking ahead of me, Lily and Baby, and eventually went off and did their own thing. Ava and Eva were older and they weren't into getting on the rides and playing games, they were there to hang out with friends.

The only thing I liked to do at the county fair was ride the bumper cars, eat cotton candy, candy apples and fries with vinegar...in that order. It didn't take long for me to get bored with the county fair, because once you walked around the massive circle of rides, games and food, there was nothing more to do but people watch. Me, Lily and Baby spent most of our time at the county fair eating, and by the time we were stuffed, we walked it off all the way back to Granny Carter's house.

When we got home Aunt Simone was waiting to give me and Aunt Baby our baths and put us to bed. She never let us stay up late, and her routine was strict: eat, bathe, bed and every bath included lots of Vaseline on your face and body! Aunt Simone and her two sons had moved back in with Granny Carter once Mama moved into Townhouse Village, so Granny's house was under Aunt Simone's control most of the time while Granny was at work, and even when Granny was home everyone knew Aunt Simone was the boss and what she said goes. Even though Aunt Simone was mean, the way she cared for us was proof of her love. I really loved Granny's new house and I begged her to let me move in so that I could attend Webber Elementary school with Aunt Baby and my cousin Anthony, but there was no extra room for me, so back to C.C. Coulter I go for fourth grade.

School is back in session and so far my fourth grade teacher Mrs. Godwin was pretty cool and I liked her because she was nice. I am usually one of the first students to complete assignments, so Mrs. Godwin let me do other things in the classroom to help her, like organize our learning center, collect book orders, pass out papers, etc. She even helped me become a Safety Patrol Officer and a Girl Scout. My social life is busy and I'm always hanging out at my Aunt Jewel's with my baby cousin Calik, or with Skyy and the neighborhood kids doing something whether it's going to a school or church function, recreation center, or participating in a talent show...age nine is treating me fine. God answered my prayers and my Mama Uncle's stepson Percy never babysit us again.

In other news, home life is going well and our road trips back and forth to Jaxson State Penitentiary to visit my Uncle Julius have become the norm. During our last visit to see Uncle Julius, Mama was introduced to Uncle Julius' prison buddy Bobby Atkinson, and next thing I know Mama and Bobby are dating so her visits to the prison become more frequent.

I was a bit confused as to why Mama would date someone who is in prison, because it didn't make sense to me. I thought dating is supposed to be romantic, where a guy sweeps you off your feet with surprise dinners and getaways or flowers and candy or a random gift of jewelry or stunning dress. My first thought is what if Mama get serious about this dude...how is a prisoner going to provide for my Mama and her three kids and will we have to start going to the prison more to visit him.

My thoughts jinxed me and the news pierced me right in the heart when Mama announced that she and Bobby were getting married after dating for only three months. This was the first decision Mama made that was truly a disappointment to me because I felt like she should have talked to me and my brothers about it first to see how we felt, and explain certain things to us like why is Mr. Bobby in prison, when does he get out and does he have any kids. Well Mama must of heard my thoughts because she made plans for us to meet our soon to be stepdad Mr. Bobby before the wedding.

I take one final look in the mirror before leaving the women's bathroom at Jaxson State Penitentiary to make sure I don't need to brush my hair or floss my teeth before my first visit with Mr. Bobby, but I must of taken too long when I heard "Come on Miracle let's go!" said Mama. I thought me, Alex and Lokey were going to meet Mr. Bobby all at once, but Mama changed her mind and decided that I would meet her fiancé first. I guess if he wins me over, then I can sell this marriage idea to my brothers. Usually when Mama and I go to the visiting room, we have to wait for the guards to bring the prisoner to the visiting room and then we find an area with enough seating, but not on this visit. To my surprise Mama grabbed me by the hand and we headed directly near the seats where visitors take pictures and took our seats, so I thought maybe we were about to take some pictures while we wait on Mr. Bobby to join us.

I thought Mama and I were waiting for the visitors ahead of us to finish their prison photo shoot, and then she and I would take pictures with Mr. Bobby, so while Mama sat there and waited, I headed over to the vending machine for some snacks. When I returned Mama was sitting there talking with some dude and I walked up and said, "Mama what's taking Mr. Bobby so long." "Hi little lady you must be Miracle, it's nice to meet you." says the dude before Mama can answer my question. Instead of responding with a "Hi" or "Hello" I looked the dude up and down then I realized he was the dude taking the pictures. "Miracle this is Mr. Bobby Atkinson," said Mama and without thinking I said very loudly, "Mama you're marrying **The Picture Man**!" Mr. Bobby immediately starts laughing and says, "Girl you are cute and funny, we're going to get along just fine." Turns out Mr. Bobby Atkinson was alright because he was very nice and he was interested in my school achievements, dreams and goals. He even asked me questions about Alex and Lokey, the things they like to do and they're schooling. Mr. Bobby assured me that my brothers and I didn't have to worry about anything and he promised to take good care of our family. I didn't ask him how he would do that behind bars, I just had to wait and see.

Early 1977 mama became Mrs. Bobby Atkinson. Once Mama and Mr. Bobby were married, it was like Mama hit the lottery, because we were getting a lot of new stuff every week; like new clothes, shoes, toys, bikes, video games, TVs, etc. I thought maybe Mr. Bobby being the picture man was paying off until the one night I was awakened by a loud pounding sound coming from downstairs.

As I made my way downstairs, I could smell the funny cigarettes as I headed down the stairs, and as I got closer to the bottom of the staircase I could see LOTS of marijuana on the table, a sewing machine, some small plastic packaging and a K-Mart bag in one of the chairs. Mama's head was down and she was pounding on something with a hammer, but she looked up just in time to meet me at the bottom of the stairs and tried to send me back to my room, but I used my "dire thirst" scheme so I could get an understanding of what was really going on. Mama said with frustration in her voice, "Ok Miracle get your water and go back to bed while Mama finish working." Then she headed to the half bathroom right across from the kitchen. I went to the kitchen sink, turned on the water and pretended to fill my cup, but in Mama's absence, I quickly ran into the dining room to see what Mama was working on and I couldn't believe my eyes! It looked like a weed manufacturing plant had been birthed in our dining room.

The hammer was lying on top of a small plastic package-containing weed that had been smashed flat by the hammer I assume. I decided to see if I could help Mama with her work and maybe negotiate a part time position in her business. I guess Mama finally heard the pounding as she rushed out of the bathroom yelling, "Miracle what are you doing put that hammer down and get away from this table!" "Mama I know you smoke weed, so that cat has been out of the bag. Let me help you get this done, I promise I won't tell anybody, I'm good at keeping secrets." I responded in my very mature, (I need in on this hustle voice).

Mama saw that I had put together fifteen plastic packages while she was in the bathroom, but the thought of me doing the weed smashing didn't sit well with her, so she said, "You can help me with the jackets." Mama showed me how to use the seam ripper to rip the lining of the jackets, then I glued the plastic packages to the lining and Mama used her sewing machine to attach the lining back to the jacket. As I pulled another jacket out of the K-Mart bag to get started ripping the lining, Mama said, "No don't rip that one, it has to be mailed."

I didn't ask Mama any questions about her weed business; I just watched and took notes. A couple of days had passed since I helped Mama with her jacket project, and it was visiting day for us at Jaxson State Penitentiary. I noticed Mama was wearing one of the jackets from the K-Mart bag but I wasn't sure which one Mama was wearing because now that I think about it the jackets were the SAME.

The guards called our name and we headed to toward the prison bars and I had a bad feeling in my spirit so I started shivering and saying, "Mama it's cold in here, I need your jacket, I'm freezing!" Mama removed her jacket while looking me in the eye and said, "Miracle don't rip my jacket like you did the other night!" In that moment I knew I was about to smuggle drugs into the Jaxson State Penitentiary at age nine.

Confession #12

Head on Collision

My, my, my time sure does fly when you're having FUN! Where did 1977 go that fast? It's all blur because life was GREAT! Mama's drug smuggling business was booming, and she had graduated from Delta College. Alex and I had reunited with our paternal grandmother Marsha because my Daddy was incarcerated and my Granny Marsha stood up in the gap to make sure Alex and I maintained a relationship with our Daddy's side of the family. Our visits to her home and with Daddy's side of the family became more frequent on holidays and birthdays. My younger brother Lokey's daddy Calvin Mack had always been in Lokey's life, but the older Lokey got, the more time he spent with his daddy's side of the family as well.

No sooner than Mama married "the picture man" Mr. Bobby, she divorced Mr. Bobby in the early part of 1978 and ended up with a Mexican boyfriend who Aunt Simone called Mexican Dan and he was the spitting image of the scary "Doritos Man" from the Doritos commercial. Not only would dating Dan Ortiz make this Mama's most disappointing decision, in my opinion, but bringing that menace into our lives was the beginning of my disdain for my Mama.

It was near the end of summer in 1978 and by this time Mama had let Dan move in with us, and ironically Mama was also taking karate classes during this time. Each week after class, Mama would come home and teach my brothers and me the karate moves she learned in class and this went on until she graduated with a yellow belt in karate.

At first I thought Mama's new boyfriend had a split personality, because most of the time he seemed nice and even generous when he gave us money or cooked for us. Then there were times he was mean as a bull. It didn't take long for me to figure out that Dan had a drinking problem, which made him violent and brought forth his many despicable behaviors. It wasn't long before he started beating Mama and trying to have sex with me.

The first time Dan was inappropriate with me, I was totally caught off guard. Dan and Mama were leaving to go somewhere and I was in the half bathroom downstairs of our apartment, which is close to the front door. Mama had already left and gotten in the car to wait on Dan, and as I was coming out of the bathroom as Dan was heading toward the front door, but he stopped right in front of me, grabbed my face and kissed me on the mouth then tried to stick his tongue in my mouth. It was so disgusting and his breath smelled awful like alcohol. "Stop it what are you doing, that's nasty ugh your breath stank!" I said. Dan pushed me against the wall and tried to stick his hands down my pants while saying, "I want your pussy!" "Leave me alone or I'm going to tell my Mama!" I cried. "Say one word to anyone and I will kill you, your Mama and your brothers!" Dan replied as he rushed out of the door to join my Mama in the car.

I retreated to my room all shook up with a sick feeling in my stomach and I was as confused as to why this was happening to me. What did I do? Am I fass? What can I do? These were the questions in my head as I tried to figure out how to handle the situation, and I kept coming back to do nothing and give it to God. I figured God answered my prayers in that situation with Percy and I have to believe he will answer my prayers about Dan. I just cried and cried until I was all cried out. Since music was my feel better go to, I cranked the radio volume on my boom box, danced and tried forget all about what just happened with Dan. When "Good Times" by Chic came blaring through the speakers, I started doing the "Bump" with my invisible friend and was dancing and creating a happy moment to make my sadness end.

It's the beginning of fall in 1979 and Mama decided she was tired of apartment living and wanted to move into a house and within two weeks before school started, nine eleven Atwater Street was our new address and also a place where many emergencies would occur. I was devastated that I had to leave all my friends and start over at a new junior high school, because I was looking forward to attending Webber Junior High school, which was considered better than Central Junior High school based on demographics.

Mama was still with Dan, so he moved into the new

house with us and things only got worse. He was still beating Mama and molesting me. Every time he touched me I wanted to tell my Mama but I was so scared that he might kill us. The only time Dan could molest me is when we were alone and it was always after he'd been drinking, so I started to stay away from home more and whenever I was alone with him, I had learned how to use reverse psychology on him and manipulate the situation to work in my favor. Sometime I would pretend to drink with him, but actually pour my drink out and let him get drunk until he passed out.

Dan molesting me had been going on for over a year at this point and was limited to fondling, but still I knew what Dan was doing to me was wrong, and I hated every encounter with him because it made me feel sick, dirty, perverted and guilty. All I could do was try to control when it happened and how far to let it go, because I just didn't have the guts to tell my Mama that her Mexican boyfriend liked eleven year olds.

September 4, 1979 was my first day as a seventh grader at Central Junior High school and I was so excited to make new friends. As I made my way through the cafeteria and hallways of Central Junior High, I was people watching and looking for familiar faces when I heard someone yell, "Miracle Carter!" and sure enough, it was my black "white" friend Monie Nelson from the projects who I met on my first prison ride. She still look the same; cute and chunky. Me and Monie exchanged phone numbers and agreed to call each other to catch up and then we both rushed off our homeroom classes.

It seems I just can't escape bullies, and for this reason, I was nearly expelled from Central Junior High on the first day. Who knew that wearing a white turtleneck shirt while flat chest would cause bullying? I didn't, but my classmate Keon Jones who sat behind me in our first hour algebra class started humiliating me in front of the class by pointing out how flat chest I was, and saying things like, "Yo titties still on summer break" or "You're in the itty bitty titty committee." The entire classroom erupted with laughter and I was so embarrassed and hurt. Not to mention it was a classroom filled with black kids from the hood, and our white algebra teacher Mr. Sonka could not control his classroom, so the laughter continued until I took matters into my own hands, literally!

I got up from my desk and went to sharpen my pencil because I thought if I wasn't sitting in front of Keon for a few minutes he would calm down or at least start picking on someone else, but nope he got up and followed me and continued to pick on me. Keon Jones was about a foot shorter than me so why he decided it was cool to follow me to the pencil sharpener and continue his bullying and taunting was beyond me. Short or not, I didn't feel comfortable with him standing behind me, so when we arrived at the pencil sharpener, I stepped to the side and said you go first.

The minute Keon stepped in front of that pencil sharpener; I was like a ninja with my hand action! I knocked the cover off the pencil sharpener, grabbed Keon by the back of his head and bashed his face into the pencil sharpener so hard and fast he dropped to the floor, but not before his blood splattered all over my white turtleneck. I looked at him lying on the floor hollering in pain, in a fetal position holding his face, and I leaned down and said, "My hands ain't on summer break punk!"

My Uncle Julius once said, "Miracle you can sell ice to an Eskimo." I had no idea what that meant and I didn't think I would ever understand what that phrase meant since I didn't see Alaska in my near or distant future. In a calm and fatherly like voice our principal Mr. White asked, "Miracle can you tell me what happened between you and Keon?" In the sweetest and best ice selling voice ever I replied, "Sir it's like I told my teacher Mr. Sonka, I'm not use to these new shoes and I was walking too fast going to the pencil sharpener and I tripped and fell into Keon, and he hit the pencil sharpener and fell to the floor." Turns out Uncle Julius was right and either Mr. White was part Eskimo or my gift to gab simply persuaded Mr. White that because of my new shoes, what happened to Keon was merely an accident.

It's been about a month since I've been at Central Junior High school and to keep my life normal like other twelve year olds; my focus is to get involved in as many extracurricular activities as possible. Student council and cheerleading were at the top of my list, but somehow I missed cheerleading tryouts, but I made it to pom-pom tryouts and the Captain of the Pom-Pom team was my new neighbor Cali Buggs. I was briefly introduced to Cali when we first became neighbors, but we hadn't hung out yet. I'm sure since our mama's were acquaintances my

Mama probably asked Cali to look after me, and the first thing I thought was I hope Cali doesn't turn out to be like Sadie. I didn't feel anything bad in my spirit about Cali. She was very pretty and two years older than me, and she had a black "white" friend too named Tamia Thomas who was the Co-Captain of the Pom-Pom team.

When I arrived to the school gym for pom-pom tryouts, Cali and Tamia were teaching the eager young ladies a routine to Michael Jackson's "Working Day and Night." The dance routine seemed easy enough and I did alright with my tryout, but Cali said I was too stiff and she would work with me so could make the team. That was a clear indication Cali liked me and that we'd become friends.

After pom-pom tryouts me, Cali and Tamia walked home together and since Cali and I were neighbors we took a route that would get Tamia home first. As we were walking, Cali and Tamia started smoking one of those funny cigarettes like Mama smoked as if they were grown women, and then out of the blue Cali said, "Miracle hit this weed!" "I don't know how to smoke weed." I replied.

Cali begin to demonstrate how to inhale a joint, she said, "Puff the joint like this, and let a little smoke out of your mouth slowly, then suck it back in and swallow. Here try it!" Cali handed me the joint and I hit that joint like an expert, which led Cali and Tamia to believe it wasn't my first time smoking. Shortly after I smoked that joint, I started turning flips and laughing for no reason, and I got paranoid and started yelling, "I can't feel my legs, why can't I feel my legs?"

Cali and Tamia started to panic when they saw my reaction to the weed, so we all decided to chill at Tamia's house and practice on the pom-pom routine to help me calm down. It must have been the weed that put some confidence in my dance moves, because I was killing the pom-pom routine to the point I was able to convince the

Captain and Co-Captain aka Cali and Tamia to change the beginning of the pom-pom routine with a dance move I created.

Once I was able execute the pom-pom routine flawlessly, me and Cali left Tamia's and headed to our neck of the woods. During our walk home Cali said, "Miracle never mess with any drugs that will over power your mind or your body." "I won't but I really liked the way that weed made me feel." I replied. "I could tell when you started doing them round house flips." Cali said as she busted out in laughter.

It must have been around five o'clock pm when I made it home after hanging out with Cali and Tamia. Dan was passed out on the couch, and based on the small empty liquor bottle I saw lying on the floor near the couch I assumed he was dead drunk. On the coffee table was his wallet, a couple of scratch off lottery tickets, and a white pack of zigzag papers. I quietly tip-toed over to the coffee table to see if there was any money in his wallet that I might need to pay for my pom-pom uniform, and just as I stuffed the eighty dollars in my pocket and turned to leave, the monster arose from his drunken nap.

Dan grabbed me by my waist and pulled me down on his lap, and I could feel his manhood rising through my pants. I don't if it was me being high off the weed but feeling his manhood rubbing vigorously against me this time was different and I felt my body beginning to betray me, so I stuck my finger down my throat and made myself vomit. The entire living room smelled of vomit and the mess it made was so overwhelming, Dan pushed me off his lap in frustration, and yelled, "Clean that shit up before your Mama comes home!"

I cleaned up the mess in the living room, and decided to keep on the same clothes I was wearing until Mama got home. The most Dan had done to me at this point was fondling, but this encounter with Dan scared me because

I didn't understand what was happening to my body and I had to tell my Mama before things went too far.

I could see headlights shine through our living room window. When I looked out of the window and saw my Granny's red chevette in the driveway, I knew it was my Mama and I was so anxious to unburden myself of this secret, but Mama never came in the house, instead Dan left the house and got into the car with Mama and they drove off.

I was so confused about everything that just happened between Dan and I. My mind was playing tricks on me from the weed I had smoked earlier and I was so paranoid that I felt like I was having an outer body experience. I started going through my Mama's bedroom like a crazy person looking for her gun because if I killed Dan, I would not have to worry about him molesting me anymore or threatening me with killing my Mama or my brothers because he would be dead.

151

"Miracle let's make some tacos." Alex said, as he made his way into our Mama's bedroom to see what I was doing. "Get out of my room!" I screamed. "This isn't your room though." Alex replied. "Uh I can't stand you, come on let's go make tacos smart ass!" I replied. To be honest I was glad to see Alex and relieved I did not find my Mama's gun.

My brothers and I ate our infamous tacos, and then we settled down in the living room with our popcorn to watch to "The Omen". I couldn't focus on the movie because my mind was still on talking to Mama about Dan and the abuse. Hours had passed since Mama and Dan left the house and my spirit was uneasy because it wasn't like Mama to be gone for such a long time without checking in on us. The phone rang and before I could say hello, my Aunt Simone said, "Miracle your Mama and Mexican Dan have been in a **Head on Collision**."

Confession #13:

Drama Queen

It was three years ago when I received that alarming phone call about Mama and Dan being in a head on collision, and my first thought upon my receipt of that call was I hope that "child molester" is dead, but then I felt agony in my soul as I hung up the phone. Tears begin to pour down my face and I knew in order for God to hear and answer my prayers for my Mama's life to be spared, I needed forgiveness in my heart, so I immediately begin to pray and ask God to spare Mama and Dan's lives. Granny Carter always said to give God his word back and it won't return void. John 15:7 says, "If you abide in me, and my words abide in you, ask whatever you wish, and it will be done for you." This was my prayer and God heard me and he spared my Mama and her Mexican boyfriend.

While Mama was recovering from the car accident, I told my Granny about the sexual abuse I had experienced during the years Dan lived with us. I told my Granny how I was going to tell Mama, but because of the car accident I didn't get the chance and I wanted to wait until Mama had fully recovered from the accident before I tell her about the abuse. Well Granny didn't wait another minute before she picked up that phone to call my Mama and share the details of our conversation.

I felt that getting my Granny involved is why Mama seemed so frustrated about the situation but I was so confused about her anger toward me. I'm sure Dan tried to convince Mama that I was a liar, but she knew in her spirit I was telling the truth and I have to believe that's why she ended their relationship. I often wondered if Mama really believed me or did she feel obligated to break up with Dan because my Granny was involved.

I remember Mama asking me what happened and why I never told her about the abuse, but I didn't want to talk about it in detail, because it was emotional and talking about it made me angry, shame, guilty, dirty and sick to my stomach. I told her it had been going on since the day Dan came into our lives, and the last time was the day of the car accident, which is when I was finally going to tell her, but I didn't get the chance.

This abuse situation with Dan hurt my Mama and I could tell because it broke our bond. Even though I was young, I watched my Mama go through so much over the years, trying to live up to my Granny's expectation, being a single mom, and giving her loving heart to men who always tend to betray her. I believe me sharing my abuse with my Granny rather than my Mama was another form of betrayal in Mama's eyes.

The trauma of sexual abuse and the impact of it had indeed changed me as a person, and it seemed like overnight I went from being a sweet, loving and happy little girl to an emotionless shell of person who learned to internalize my pain and put up walls. The abuse also changed my relationship with my Mama because I was harboring so much anger inside toward her, and I felt like it was her fault that Dan was able to do what he did.

In 1980 at age thirteen I was mentally damaged from the abuse. My body was going through changes and my mental stability was being challenged. My mind played tricks on me and I often felt like people could see the trauma and that made me feel insecure like I didn't fit in with certain people or I wasn't worthy to be loved by certain people.

My solution was to develop a coping mechanism that would ultimately help me forget about the dysfunction I had experienced between the ages of nine to twelve. Therefore, I created two versions of Miracle, which was Miracle the "overachiever" and Miracle the "social butterfly". Being an "overachiever" was natural and didn't take much effort because it's who I was born to be, but being a "social butterfly" took lots of effort because I had to learn how to mask my trauma and protect my vulnerability.

In school and in the presence of my family I was Miracle the "overachiever" smart, happy, and funny with a high-energy personality. In the hood aka the streets I was Miracle the "social butterfly" who mingled with any and everybody and could relate to people no matter what level they were on. I made friends with the people in school who were "book" smart like me and I learned plenty from the ones who lived in my hood and were "street" smarter than me. Identifying and mastering my two personalities, gave me the balance I needed to be successful in school and to survive in the inner city ghetto.

During my early teens the "overachiever" in me had accomplished being on student council, I was on both the Pom-Pom and Cheerleading teams, I won a public speaking award, I was a track star and ultimately ranked number three of my overall graduating class. The "social butterfly" in me snagged the cutest boys, became friends with the most popular people, and my bubbly personality undeniably made me the life of any party.

It was during mid school year of eighth grade for me when our immediate family moved to Buena Vista and I transferred from Central Junior High to attend Ricker Middle School for a couple of short months and then went on to Buena Vista High School for my freshman year and the beginning of my sophomore year. During 1981-1982 my life was somewhat normal and I was started to feel good about my life again. Living in Buena Vista, was a blessing because I was introduced to a whole other demographic of black people than what I was use to, meaning the majority of the population in Buena Vista were middle class black folks. I was embraced my people who had a better lifestyle than I did, and this exposure afforded me the opportunity of going on more social outings and getting involved in church again. Even though I accepted Christ as my savior at a very young age, while living in Buena Vista, Karia Holden who had been one of my best friends since eighth grade was a preacher's daughter. It was through my friendship with Karia, that I joined her father's church and I returned to Christ, where I sang in the choir and led my first song "I Love the Lord".

In 1982 I turned fifteen and by now I had mastered my two identities. I had blocked the trauma of sexual abuse from my mind so that I could continue to excel in school and have a normal social life, but as usual, when everything in my life is going well something always happens to change the course of my fate.

In the fall of 1982 we moved back into the inner city ghetto on Warren Street and I would become a classmate to the graduating Class of 1985 as a sophomore at Saginaw High School. Even though most of the people in my graduating class probably remembered me from seventh grade and maybe a couple of them remembered me from elementary, the fact is I spent two years in another school district, so I had to start over and make new friends yet again.

First thing I thought about when I started school at Saginaw High was reuniting with the girls from my former cheerleading squad at Central Junior High, so I went to try outs, but I was rejected by the girls right away. My spirit was burdened the minute I walked away from the tryouts in tears, and my spirit finally broke. All I knew for certain is that I never wanted to feel that kind of rejection from anyone ever again. It didn't matter that I was good person who loved God, the fact is I was not good enough and no matter how smart, funny, or cute I believed I was, as long as I lived in the ghetto or on the wrong side of the tracks, I would never be good enough to fit in with certain people.

During the first week of attending Saginaw High, I came into contact with several girls I remembered from Central Junior High but unfortunately many of them acted like they didn't remember me or that I wasn't on their level so they had no interest in being friends with me. I was so happy to reconnect with my childhood friend from the projects Monie Nelson, and to be honest, she was really the only girl at Saginaw High who embraced me. Monie and I cliqued, became the best of friends and were pretty much inseparable from the day we reconnected in our sophomore year.

Even though I was rejected by the Cheerleading squad, I did not give up on my first love which was acting. Drama was one of my electives each year and I loved it so much I joined the Drama Club. My drama teacher Ms. Vargas was one of my favorite high school teachers because she believed in my acting skills and always pushed me passed my potential. Whenever Ms. Vargas gave me a role that challenged me, I would whine and sometimes throw a tantrum and Ms. Vargas would look at me and say with laughter, "Miracle you are such a **Drama Queen**."

It was my love for acting and the drama club that kept me focused all three years of high school. I felt because I was able to hold a leading role in every play, Hollywood was my fate and someday I'd become a famous actress. Unfortunately, one awful day during my senior year in high school, I was forced into my own REAL LIFE horror and that horrific experience would forever change the trajectory of my life!

Confessions #14:

Where's the Bathroom

Cedrick Persons was a classmate who made an appearance at Saginaw High school aka the "High" almost every day but never went to class. Instead he was busy being a thug in the streets and holding high rank with the Crazy Boyz. One day as I was heading into the first floor bathroom at the "High" Cedrick felt the need to approach me and say, "I thought you were different, but you ain't nothing but a bathroom queen!" At the "High" a bathroom queen could be defined as a female who spent most of her time skipping classes to hang out in the girls' bathroom to get high and drunk.

It's the middle of first semester during our senior year at Saginaw High when Monie frantically approached me at our school locker we shared and says, "Miracle our name has been removed from the senior list!" "Girl I don't care, come on let's go sell a couple nickel bags of weed to these bathroom queens and hit seven eleven." I replied.

Soon as Monie and I walked into the first floor bathroom we ran into our archenemies Carmen Love and her girl Erica White, but we ignored them as we leaned against the wall and smoked a joint. I sold a few nickel bags of weed to a couple of the bathroom queens, but as Monie and I left the bathroom, I felt in my spirit trouble would find us when we returned to the school. While we're shopping around at seven eleven I tell Monie that I have a feeling all hell is going to break loose when we return to school, but Monie is too busy grabbing our favorites; burrito, Doritos, lemon heads, watermelon and sour apples now & later candy and mixed slurpee. After a ten-minute delay, Monie asked "Why you think that?" "My spirit has me feeling like either Carmen or Erica is going to snitch on us." I replied

As Monie and I rushed back into the school and headed toward our locker, we heard, "Miracle Carter and Monie Nelson stop right there!" It was the voice of our Assistant Principal Mr. Baxter calling our names. Monie and I took off running trying to get to our locker and clean it out before getting busted for the liquor that was stashed in there, but soon as I opened the locker, the fifth of Seagram's Gin fell and broke on the floor, and by then Mr. Baxter had caught up to us and we were busted! Mr. Baxter escorted Monie and me to the office and both Monie and I were suspended from Saginaw High school for one week during second marking period, and our names had been removed from the senior list.

Monie and I decided not to tell our mama's we were suspended from school, so during our suspension we pretended to attend school, but instead we would meet up and head over to the Crazy Boyz house to hang out with Carlos Hughes and Jay Sears, who were both known gang members of the Crazy Boyz. The Crazy Boyz was a local gang of young thugs who were known for gang banging and selling drugs. I was kicking it with Jay; and Carlos was digging on Monie, so they told us we could hang out with them at the Crazy Boyz house for the entire week of our suspension.

The Crazy Boyz house was the home of Evan Davis' daddy and it's where the gang members used to hang with each other and with their girls. I had heard Evan Davis could be sexually aggressive, but I'd never seen that side of him whenever Jay and I would hang out at the house, which wasn't often, in fact most time I'd ever been at the Crazy Boyz house is when Monie and I were suspended.

One morning during our school suspension as I was walking toward the bus stop. I saw one of the Crazy Boyz cars that Jay usually drove coming up the street toward me. I thought it was Jay, but as the car got closer, slowed down and rolled down the tinted window, I saw that it was Evan driving. I hadn't yet noticed if Jay was in the car with Evan because I immediately starting dancing in the street when I heard the sounds of Run DMC blaring from the kicker box rapping:

"I'm the king of rock, there is none higher Sucker MC's should call me sire to burn my kingdom, you must use fire I won't stop rockin' till I retire. Now we rock the party and come correct our cuts are on time and rhymes connect got the right to vote and will elect and other rappers can't stand us, but give us respect!"

Evan turned down the music and said "Hey Miracle."

"Hey bro what's up where's Jay?" I responded. "That lazy nigga at the crib, and I told him I was going to pick up my girl, so he asked me to stop by and pick you up too." Evan replied. "Crank that radio back up bro!" I said to Evan as I jumped in the car without hesitation. Evan cranked up the radio while handing me a joint and as we smoked, we started rapping along with Run DMC in unison.

When we arrived to the Crazy Boyz house, Evan jumps out of the car and goes to open the trunk of the car and tells me the side door to the house is unlocked and to go on in the house. I immediately started feeling paranoid from the weed. Once I was inside of the house my paranoia got worse because it's so quiet throughout the house and it dawned on me that Evan said Jay asked him to pick me up because he was going to pick up his girlfriend, and now that I was inside the house I don't see his girlfriend or Jay. As I called out for Jay, I'm startled by Evan's sudden presence when I hear him say, "He's in the middle bedroom probably high as hell and passed out." I tried to stay calm and act normal as I say to Evan, "Bro go wake his ass up!"

I sat on the couch, grabbed the TV remote and turned on the television while Evan went into middle bedroom only to come right back into the living room and say, "Miracle Jay wants you in there with him." As I stood up and walked toward that middle bedroom my tears begin to pour because I knew Jay was not in that bedroom, and the second my hand touched that doorknob, I was right when I felt Evan Davis push the barrel of his gun into my lower back and say, "Take off your clothes!"

I screamed and cried and begged Evan not to make me take my clothes off and not to hurt me. Evan put his gun to my head and said, "Don't make me hurt you, I actually like you Miracle, but if you don't take off your clothes and give me what I want and quit crying, you're going to make me hurt you." Evan Davis raped me and held a gun to my head the entire time and threatened to pull the trigger if I didn't stop crying. I'm not sure if I wanted to DIE, and that's why I cried louder and harder, or if I thought by crying louder and harder it would stop Evan from raping me, but me crying louder and harder didn't do either. Evan didn't pull the trigger and he didn't stop raping me!

When it was finally over I felt my soul leave my body and then I heard Evan tell me to get dressed. I was shaking uncontrollably and still crying, so Evan threatened me again and said, "Shut the fuck up with all that damn crying. You know you liked it and you wanted it! If you tell anybody, I'm going to kill you, your Mama and your brothers." Then Evan dropped me off at home, and I immediately ran a hot bath and scrubbed my body over and over and over, but the horror and the trauma were etched in my mind. From that day on I never again spoke to Jay or any of the other Crazy Boyz, and I didn't tell anyone that Evan Davis was a rapist.

Monie and I are back in school from our one week

suspension, and of course our names were still removed from senior list, and to make matters worse for me, Mrs. Vargas wouldn't allow me to participate in the drama club until my name was back on the senior list and my grade point was at least a three point. Neither Monie nor I was in no mood to deal with the reality we might not graduate with the Class of 1985, so we did our usual, which was skipping classes to go get high and drunk and forget about our real life issues.

Somehow on this particular day Monie and I ended up downtown near a bunch of office buildings and we both needed to use the bathroom, so went into the first building we saw. When we walked into the building there were two or three men walking around in military looking suits and one was Black, so I asked him **"Where's The Bathroom?"** he pointed and replied, "Around that corner on the right."

When Monie and I came out of the restroom the Black military dude was waiting in the hallway, and greeted me with a handshake as he introduced himself. "Hi I'm

Sergeant Jones." he said. "Hi I'm Miracle and this is my best friend Monie." I replied. "Why aren't you young ladies in school?" Sergeant Jones asked. "Because we had to use the bathroom!" I replied and Monie I started laughing and begin walking away. "Wait a minute let me talk to you about your future and your plans after high school." said Sergeant Jones. There was something fatherly about Sergeant Jones' voice that made me trust him enough to peak my interest in what he had to say, so I listened.

Two hours after meeting Sergeant Jones, I had taken an aptitude test for the United States Army and my score was so impressive that Sergeant Jones drove me and Monie back to the school and he voluntarily met with my high school counselor to share my test results and discuss my future. Sergeant Jones worked with my high school counselor and developed an academic plan that would get my name back on the senior list, get me back in the drama club, and get me to walk across that stage in June and get my high school diploma.

Sergeant Jones insisted on driving me home to meet my Mama and speak with her about everything that happened earlier that day. He wanted to share the results of my aptitude test, meeting with my high school counselor to develop an academic plan that will get me back on track for graduation, and most importantly to convince Mama into letting me to join the United States Army after graduation.

Sergeant Jones was one of the most influential people in my life during one the darkest times of my life. The simple fact that he cared about my future gave me a glimpse of hope and helped me rediscover a piece of that little girl my Mama named "Miracle."

Epilogue

When Mama moved our family back into the inner city in 1982 and I started Saginaw High as a sophomore, I never imagined Miracle "the rebel" would exist. I imagined my senior year would be a time of happiness and celebration, for all the many accomplishments I would have made throughout my high school education. Surely that should have been easy for me since I was an "overachiever" and "social butterfly" but instead my attitude toward life, and my social behavior became increasingly negative, and my life rapidly spiraled out of control.

Fact is, my new neighborhood and social circle was an influence of drugs, sex, alcohol, violence and crime; and as a result it was just a matter of time before my daydreams became nightmares, my ambition turned into manipulation, and my thoughts became cold calculated schemes. Between the ages of fifteen to seventeen, I was rebelling against my Mama and held a lot of anger in my heart toward her because I was convinced that my Mama's choice in men was her weakness and that weakness was the primary source of dysfunction that continuously impacted our lives. Not only was I angry at Mama, but the rage I held in my heart toward my Daddy was a whole other issue. It was indeed fair to say I hated him because not only was he in and out of prison over the years, but when he did get out of prison, he moved away to another city and started a life with a woman and her two sons.

My rebellion coupled with all of this anger and rage brought about the birth of a "new" Miracle who was convinced that selling drugs, running the streets with gang members, and hustling older men, would lead the way out of poverty. When the reality was I lived in the hood, so not only did I limit myself to hanging out with people in the hood, I also begin to adopt a hood mentality of thinking I had to do whatever was necessary to survive in the hood. By the time I turned seventeen the "Miracle" I once knew and loved was long gone and I had lost all hope of her ever coming back.

In early 1985 Mama got remarried to Thomas Ruffin, who was considered a "bad boy" in the streets. I felt like Mama was too old and too good for Thomas, and I didn't feel comfortable with the fact that Thomas was only twenty-six years old, which made him nine years older than me. Thomas was a bully and I didn't trust him because of the way he looked at me, or the things I heard about him in the streets. I actually begin to hate Thomas because he brought so much dysfunction into our home. Thomas beat on my

Mama whenever he felt like it, which caused us to leave our home and flee to safety more than I can count, and I remember one time his abuse toward Mama was so bad that I ran away from home for at least one month before I returned home. The rage I would feel whenever Thomas was in my presence scared me, so I avoided him and his bullying as much as I could, because I didn't trust the "new" Miracle.

Finally it's a few days before my senior high school graduation and my life is back on track and things seem to be going well for me. I just finished my last performance in the play "Arsenic and Old Lace" where I held the role of Elaine who was the fiancé of Mortimer. I was also preparing for an upcoming outing with Sergeant Jones and some of the other Army recruits to discuss our final plans for deployment to basic training. Mama also decided to give me a graduation/going away party immediately following our high school graduation ceremony.

Thursday, June 6, 1985 has arrived and its graduation

day for Saginaw High's Class of 1985 and I am beside myself with excitement because I can't believe I'll be graduating from high school on Thursday and then leaving first thing Friday morning for South Carolina to enter basic training and become a soldier in the United States Army.

A little disappointment started to creep up in my spirit as I thought about leaving for the Army, because I had never imagined myself in the military, and since birth all I've ever wanted to become was a famous actress. I thought of my many conversations with Sergeant Jones, who would constantly remind me as he prepped me for this life changing transition, that after three years of service if I didn't like the military, I didn't have to reenlist. Sergeant Jones encouraged me to take advantage of the GI Bill, which was a financial benefit to help me pay for college when I leave the service. To know I had options besides staying in the inner city ghetto for the rest of my life was enough to put hope back in my spirit and a smile on my face.

Even though it was graduation day and I had a lot to be thankful for and happy about, I just couldn't shake this feeling in my spirit because it was a familiar feeling that I get whenever things are going well in my life, and then something bad always happens.

Graduation was so much fun and the entire Class of 1985 was happy, excited and loving on each other. Everyone was discussing their parties and open houses, or colleges they were attending and it was just an overall good time. I made it home from graduation and got changed out of my graduation outfit and put on an orange t-shirt that read: Class of 1985 with some jeans and waited in the dining room with some of my family members while we waited for other guests to arrive to my party. Within two hours after the graduation ceremony, my Mama's house was wall to wall with our family, some of my classmates, people from the neighborhood, some of Thomas' family and friends, and even Sergeant Jones stopped by to bring a gift. I was so happy, proud and hopeful of becoming reacquainted with Miracle "the overachiever" in my near future!

Mama finally shut the party down around ten o'clock in the evening because she and I had to make an early start in the morning. I helped Mama clean up from the party and we talked a bit, then I gave her a goodnight hug, kiss, and off to my bedroom to for sleep. As I lay in my bed it is hard for me to fall asleep because all I could think about was leaving the city I call "Sodom and Gomorrah" and never coming back. My thoughts were interrupted by my bedroom door being slightly opened and the light from the dining room shining through the cracked door, and I immediately feel rage in the pit of my stomach when I see Thomas standing on the other side of my bedroom door in his robe that is wide open and exposing all of his manhood. I continued to play possum hoping Thomas would close my door and walk away, but he just continued to stand there in my doorway, so

I shifted my body from lying on my back to facing the bedroom door, and I guess that startled Thomas so he walked into the dining room.

It was really too late in the evening for me to be going anywhere, but every fiber of my being was screaming leave NOW, so I immediately jumped out of bed closed my bedroom door, and put on the same clothes I just took off, my orange Class of 1985 t-shirt and blue jeans. I had no idea what was going on, or why Thomas was practically nude standing in my doorway, but I also had no desire to stick around and find out. I made a quick phone call to my homeboy, Chuck Miller and asked him to meet me in front of Times store in twenty minutes, and I told Chuck I would explain what was going on when I got there. When I walked into the dining room, Thomas was sitting at the dining room table with his robe hanging open and stroking his manhood into an erection. Even though I was fuming with rage, I very calmly ignored him and his behavior and walked right passed him into the kitchen. "Where are you going this time of the night?" Thomas asked. I did not respond, in fact I walked faster praying that I make it out of the back door and safely to Times store to meet Chuck.

Thirty minutes later I am sitting on Chuck's bed crying my eyes out because I am outraged and confused by Thomas' motives. Wondering if I had not left the house, what was he planning to do? I felt like Chuck was halfway listening to what I was saying because he's was too busy snorting cocaine, until he asked me between snorts, "You want me to shoot that nigga between the eyes?" "Let me snort a line." I replied. Chuck happily obliged and that would be the first time ever that I snorted cocaine. Chuck and I stayed up all night talking until he fell asleep on me. I got up from the bed and looked in one of Chuck's dresser drawers for a t-shirt to sleep in, that is when I saw his gun, and I could not help but pick it up and play with it because I had never touched a gun before.

Daylight was creeping in through Chuck's bedroom window and I knew it was time for me to head home and start getting ready for my trip to South Carolina and my new life. Chuck was knocked out sleep and I did not want to wake him up, so I decided to take his gun with me for protection, just in case, and I would return it before Mama dropped me off at Sergeant Jones' house.

The closer I got to our house the faster my heart begins to beat and I'm not sure if it's because I'm still high off the line of cocaine I did with Chuck or if I'm on a power trip because I have Chuck's gun tucked into my jeans. As I reached the corner of Twelve/Tuscola my spirit became more and more aggravated so I begin to pray, "The Lord is my shepherd; I shall not want. He maketh me to lie down in green pastures: he leadeth me beside the still waters. He restoreth my soul: he leadeth me in the paths of righteousness for his name's sake. Yea, though I walk through the valley of the shadow of death, I will fear no evil: for thou art with me; thy rod and thy staff they comfort me."

As soon as I made a right turn on to Tuscola, I could not believe my eyes and I literally froze right where I stood as the car approached the corner, slowed down and came to a stop. I continued my prayer, "Thou preparest a table before me in the presence of mine enemies: thou anointest my head with oil; my cup runneth over. Surely goodness and mercy shall follow me all the days of my life: and I will dwell in the house of the Lord forever."

Without hesitation, I pulled Chuck's gun from my jeans, I looked evil in its eyes, I aimed Chuck's gun between those evil eyes and begin shooting!